A Once Perfect Place

Also by Larry Maness

Nantucket Revenge

A Once Perfect Place

A Jake Eaton Mystery
by

Larry Maness

LYFORD
Books

Thanks to Professor Walter W. Boyd, University of Helsinki, Department of Geology, for geological and scientific research.

LYFORD Books
Published by Presidio Press
505 B San Marin Drive, Suite 300
Novato, CA 94945-1340

Library of Congress Cataloging-in-Publication Data

Maness, Larry.
    A once perfect place : a Jake Eaton mystery / Larry Maness.
      p. cm.
    ISBN 0-89141-567-X
    I. Title.
    PS3563.A465505   1996
    813'.54—dc20   96-24507
                                      CIP

Printed in the United States of America

For my parents

A Once Perfect Place

-1-

"There comes a time in life," Mildreth Gibbon Preston said, "when even on our best days we have to admit that things will not improve. Tea?"

"No, thank you," Jake said and migrated toward the four-story yellow and white dollhouse with black shutters that sat on a base of cobblestone street, brick walk, and granite curbing. A dozen miniature gas lamps lined the street. "It looks real."

"It ought to, it's an exact replica of the house we're standing in, both built in 1837. The dollhouse was made for the children of my great-great-uncle. Back then—I'm told—the children of Beacon Hill were well behaved." Mildreth Gibbon Preston checked the disapproval in her voice with a question whose answer she already knew. "Do you have children, Mr. Eaton?"

"No children," Jake said and peered through a tiny window at the porcelain dolls. The dolls seemed to be admiring the small portraits hanging from the floral papered walls. "And if I did, they wouldn't be playing with this."

"Just like my daughter and her husband. When they visit from Oregon, they're always afraid my grandchildren might break something, so they just look at it. Never touch. The rest of the time it collects dust. There are two hand-carved springer spaniels curled up by the fire in the parlor, first floor on the right."

Jake heard the command in her voice, found the room, and looked in. As she said, two carved brown and whites lay next to a painted blazing fire.

"Why didn't you bring your dog, Mr. Eaton? I expected you would."

"He can get rowdy."

"I've heard the same about you."

Jake turned away from the dollhouse. In the grayish light that poured around the storm clouds through the windows of the real house, Mildreth Gibbon Preston struck a meditative pose. Jake guessed her to be seventy, maybe seventy-five, and stubborn. She was slightly built, but seemed strong. He knew she was wealthy.

"I don't mind being looked over," he said, "but Watson gets a little nervous."

"I can't speak for your dog, but my guess is you do mind. All the more reason I appreciate your coming." She sat at one end of the camelback couch, her clear blue eyes sweeping over Jake like the needle on a meter dial. He was all she'd heard: strong and commanding and with a face that made him easy to talk to. "The pity of being old, Mr. Eaton . . . may I call you Jake?"

"Please."

"The pity of being old, Jake, is that people ignore you. Even people you know stop paying serious attention. Pretty soon they're treating you like a demented child." She lifted the teapot with a steady hand and poured herself a steaming cup. "Are you sure you wouldn't like some?" she asked.

Jake declined, wishing she'd have offered whiskey—not his normal drink, but he'd have taken it to ward off the spring chill in the room.

Mrs. Preston took a satisfying sip of tea and put down her cup. "I hate to be ignored," she said finally.

"Who doesn't?" Jake thought that nobody could ignore Mildreth Gibbon Preston for long.

"Tell that to Lieutenant Moreau of the Keene, New Hampshire, police. He's in charge of the investigation—such as it is," she said tersely. "I've tried talking to him and have gotten nowhere."

"Cops aren't famous for giving away information."

"Does the same go for you?" she asked.

Jake watched the wind whip the trees outside. "If I take a case, I keep my client informed."

Mrs. Preston stiffened. "You say that as though you have no intention of working for me." Jake's look gave nothing away. "When our mutual friend Gloria said she knew a private detective, I told her I didn't want you simply paying me a courtesy call."

"Is that what you think I'm doing?" asked Jake.

"It crossed my mind. Gloria asks you to do her a favor, and here you are."

"Now, why would I do that?"

Mrs. Preston smiled ruefully. "Even wealthy folks gossip, Jake. With all the time on our hands, we might even be better at it than most. You and Gloria are fond of each other. Everybody who knows her knows that. As I said, we love to gossip."

"Gloria and I are good friends," Jake said, uncomfortable with the direction of the conversation. "The point is, Mrs. Preston, I don't believe I can do more than the Keene police are already doing. And if I can't, I won't take your money."

"The police are bumbling fools!" Mrs. Preston snapped. "Lieutenant Moreau is bound up in red tape just like the state is. My late husband, Oliver, always said we'd strangle in red tape, and I'm beginning to believe him. You wouldn't think a simple memorial could get so complicated."

Giving the state a sizable gift of land as a memorial to her late husband never seemed simple to Jake. "I suppose it's too late to back out?" he asked.

"Assuming I wanted to, and I don't. No, backing out is not an option. If I wanted to give up, I wouldn't have asked to see you, would I?" She spoke as if she were scolding a child, and Jake's expression let her know he wasn't amused.

"All right," he said after a deep breath, "why don't you give me the details."

"As I told you," Mrs. Preston began, her voice kinder, "after my husband died two years ago, I began thinking about a memorial. What could I provide that would be a fitting tribute? Do you know much about my husband, Jake?"

Jake—like most—had heard of Oliver Preston, and reading *Who's Who* had caught him up on the details. Jake repeated them: "He was a Nobel laureate in chemistry; professor emeritus at

Harvard; founder of the Wilderness Association for Environmental Sanity; founder of World Watch, the organization that
monitors oil spills and toxic waste dumps; and the man considered by most to be the founder of the modern environmental
movement."

"Oliver was in love with the world," she said proudly. "Every
inch of it. That's why I thought an appropriate memorial would
be the property we bought years ago in New Hampshire. Oliver
loved to spend time there hiking, exploring nature. I wanted to
put a small bronze plaque with his name on it at each end of a
trail he'd cut through the land. Nothing fancy, just two simple
plaques mounted on granite and set in the ground. The only condition," Mrs. Preston emphasized, "is that it could never be developed."

"Sounds like you're just taking down 'No Trespassing' signs on
land you already own."

"Precisely. Two years ago, when Oliver died, I had the land
posted private and off-limits. It was my way of sealing off the mem-
ories, forgetting about it. Then I realized that Oliver wouldn't
appreciate my behavior, and I decided to make the land a gift to
the state."

"But why the formality?"

"Because I'm not going to live forever, and I've come to believe
that my daughter and I will never close the awful rift that exists
between us," she said without emotion. "She's made it very plain
to me that she doesn't want any of what she calls our 'family burdens'—the dollhouse, for example. It's been in our family for over
one hundred and fifty years, and she doesn't want to be responsible for it. I don't appreciate that, but I understand it. When I
die, the dollhouse will go to a local museum. I've already made
those arrangements. The land is another matter. I don't want it
sold off to some speculator who'd most likely put in a trailer park."

"Or a shopping mall."

"Equally detestable, along with a ski resort or loggers coming
in and cutting the forest. Each possibility is unsettling, so I kept
pursuing this path of giving away the land. At first, it seemed sim-

ple enough. The state wanted a title search—and proof of deed, which I have in my safe-deposit box at the bank. They also wanted a recent survey. We bought the property over forty years ago and had one done then, but it wasn't current enough. I ended up calling this man." She handed Jake a surveyor's business card with the name Colin Owens and a local address on it.

"How did you get his name?" Jake asked as the sky outside grew darker.

"Winslow, New Hampshire, is the closest village to my property. The sheriff there, Myron Sellers, called me about Mr. Owens once he'd heard of my plans for the property. I've known Myron for several years."

"Dependable?"

"Reasonably."

Jake knew the satisfaction of reaching conclusions but resisted the jump. "Why just reasonably?" he questioned.

"It's hard to say. I guess I never really trusted the man totally. I think I was never comfortable with his motives. I find him self-serving."

"Yet you hired Owens on Sellers's recommendation."

"Only after I invited Mr. Owens over and had a look at him. I know nothing about surveying property, but Owens seemed knowledgeable. He said for a parcel this size, an aerial survey would have to be done."

"How big is the parcel?" Jake asked.

"Twenty thousand acres."

Jake's brows arched. "Big."

"I prefer 'expansive,' just like Oliver's life. The memorial should fit the man, don't you think?"

What Jake thought was that Mrs. Preston was going to do what she wanted. "What else did Colin Owens tell you?" he asked.

"That the survey would have to be done immediately. He said if we waited much longer into spring when the leaves were out, all we'd get is a picture of treetops. I didn't want to wait another minute, so I hired him," she said, shifting position on the couch. "Owens rented an airplane equipped with the necessary cameras from a private airport near Keene. He went up for his second survey flight about two weeks ago, and that was the last anyone heard from him."

"People just don't disappear," Jake said.

"Colin Owens did."

"Maybe he had good reason."

"Meaning that even though I had Myron's recommendation, I may have hired the wrong person?"

Jake shrugged.

"That I didn't do my homework?"

Jake's look said it was possible.

"No, Mr. Eaton. You are forty, divorced, and the sole proprietor of the Eaton Agency since your brother was killed. You are on a retainer with one of the largest holding companies in the world, The Gorham Corporation, for whom you perform occasional investigations. You live in Cambridge with your dog and earn great respect for your ability to get the job done. If you didn't, I wouldn't have asked to meet with you. I never act precipitately. Nor do I let friends unduly influence me."

"Myron Sellers?" Jake asked.

Mrs. Preston dismissed Jake's challenge. "I was thinking more of Gloria," she said. Her tone shifted from combative to somber. "I'm worried about her, Jake. She's changed."

"Having your life threatened does that," Jake reminded her. "But she'll be all right."

"Now that you've stopped the man who tried to kill her, you mean. I'm very grateful you did. Gloria is a wonderful woman."

Jake's agreement remained silent as lightning flashed and heavy wind-driven rain splashed against the windows. "What did you find out when you checked up on Colin Owens?" Jake asked, returning to the subject at hand.

"I didn't 'check up,' as you put it. I had Myron's recommendation and very little time. I called Owens, and he was willing to visit me at my home. I hired him on the spot. What else was I to do?"

"Maybe you've done enough already," Jake offered.

Mrs. Preston stiffened. "You mean I should stay out of it?"

"I mean the police will probably find him, or when he gets tired of running around he'll come home."

"You sound just like Lieutenant Moreau, telling me in not so many words to mind my own business." She put down her teacup and stood, looking Jake straight in the eyes. "Moreau thinks I'm a meddling old fool when all I'm trying to do is help. I promised Terry I would."

"Who's Terry?"

"Colin's wife. She called when Colin failed to return home, and I told her I didn't know what I could do. Then she showed up at my front door with three young children." Mildreth walked to the dollhouse and looked inside. "I guess I felt a certain obligation. After all, he was working for me when he disappeared. And," she told Jake, "I know what it's like to lose a husband. At my age, it's hard enough. I felt sorry for Mrs. Owens. She's too young to go through such sadness." Turning around to look at Jake, she said with her blue eyes burning, "I want you to find Colin Owens."

The rain had stopped by the time Jake pulled into the Commercial Wharf parking lot. He got out of his old blue Saab and walked around the back of what was once a busy Boston waterfront warehouse. Now it's four floors of offices and condos, with granite, exposed brick, and tall windows leading to stamp-sized wrought iron–wrapped balconies overlooking a small marina and Boston Harbor. Gloria Gorham—sole heir to The Gorham Corporation's fortune—had rented a slip there for *Gamecock,* her pre–World War II forty-eight-foot custom wooden sloop.

Jake used his key to unlock the security gate, then walked down the aluminum ramp toward the shining blue hull. Gloria, dressed in an orange tank top and jeans, was mopping the rain off the canvas decks when Jake climbed aboard.

"You were right about Mildreth Preston," he said, leaning against the mahogany deckhouse.

Gloria stopped mopping long enough to kiss Jake lightly on the lips. "Mildreth *Gibbon* Preston," she corrected as Watson, Jake's flop-eared cross between a black Lab and a collie raced toward him demanding attention. Watson had been belowdecks hiding from the early spring storm. Gloria watched Jake and Watson roughhouse, then went back to swabbing the deck.

"I stand corrected," Jake said. "Mildreth *Gibbon* Preston. She's quite a woman."

"I told you."

Jake watched Gloria ring out the mop and wipe down the last puddle. "Cleaning house?" he asked.

"Keeping ahead of the rot," she answered. "Fresh water running down where I can't get at it has ruined more wooden boats than all the hurricanes put together. I don't plan on it ruining mine," she said, wiping steadily along the brightly varnished toe rail of the immaculately refinished boat. When Gloria had worked her way back to the transom, she turned to Jake, a light sweat shining on her nearly white arms. In other more normal years, she'd be golden brown now. "Care for a drink?" she asked.

"Sounds better than tea."

Gloria smiled knowingly. "Mildreth's from the old school. Nothing alcoholic before six o'clock."

"So I gathered," Jake said, following her past a reclining Watson and down below.

Gloria stepped into the portside galley. Sunlight breaking through the clouds spilled down from the opened hatch and bathed her in warm light. She was thirty-four, and wearing the look of someone locked in a dungeon with all the cheerless indignities that a dark, damp hole could offer. But she hadn't been locked up, she'd been threatened by a madman with the promise of her own death. That promise, the harrowing thought that life could end in a terrifying instant regardless of how many millions of dollars she had access to, changed her. Before, life had context. She'd been head of Resorts Management, a division of The Gorham Corporation, and time revolved around five-year plans and takeovers. Now, she saw life as random and sadly out of control. Since moving aboard *Gamecock* six months ago, Gloria had been trying to get back some control.

"So, how are you doing?" Jake asked.

"I'm fine." It was a little lie that hung there while she sliced the lime and squeezed two slivers over the iced vodka. She looked over at Jake. "Daddy stopped by earlier," she said.

Daddy was F. Gordon Gorham, head of The Gorham Corporation and Jake's sometime employer. *Gamecock* had been his yacht before Gloria's narrow escape from the madman's attempt on her life. She came away from the experience more aware than ever that money has its limits, that rich people die, too. She moved aboard to isolate herself from such thoughts and decided not to get off until she was more comfortable facing the world.

"How is your father?" Jake asked.

"Fine. He was wondering the same about me."

"What'd you tell him?"

"What I always tell him," she said and handed Jake his gimlet light on the Rose's lime juice, the way they both liked it. "I'm not ready to go back to work. I don't know when I will be." She raised her glass. "Cheers."

"Cheers."

She drank and stepped past Jake. She climbed the companionway steps and sat out in the cockpit. Jake sat across from her. Watson lay between them on the cockpit floor, his attention moving from one to the other as they spoke.

"Looks like I'm going to New Hampshire for a while," Jake said.

Gloria pushed her shoulder-length light brown hair behind her ears. "Then you're taking the case?"

He nodded. "Not that there's much to it."

"Milly thinks there is."

Jake cocked his head. "'Milly,' is it?" he teased.

Gloria smiled genuinely. "I told you, I've known the Prestons for years. You know how it is. Beacon Hill and old Yankee money. You have a town house on the Hill and a summer place in the mountains. Only Oliver never built anything on his property. It was his private park."

"All twenty thousand acres."

"It was beautiful," Gloria told him.

"You've been there?"

"Often as a child. After mother died, Milly looked out for Dad and me. We were invited up to Preston Mountain several times. I'll always remember the bright swirls of fog hanging over the streams and the mossy stone walls snaking their way up the sloping woods and how clean the air was and how bright the sky seemed. I loved it." She took another sip of her drink, then bent forward to pat the black dog curled up at her feet. "Watson would love it, too," she said. "Miles and miles of tall trees and babbling brooks."

"Just the kind of place a man could get lost in," Jake noted.

"Do you think that's what happened?"

"Could be. Mrs. Preston didn't have much to tell me except that she hired a surveyor, and he disappeared doing a job for her."

"It upset her very much."

"I gathered that."

"I don't mean the man disappearing. I mean all of it. The memorial, the unwillingness of the state to accept Milly's gift graciously. It hurt her. She thinks everybody ought to respect Oliver and his memory the way she does. That's all she has, really—his memory."

Plus a million bucks, Jake thought but didn't say it. "What do you remember of Oliver?" Jake asked, sipping his drink.

Gloria thought a moment. "It was like he had antennae," she said. "That's what I remember about Oliver. He was always taking information in, processing it, and making decisions and plans before most men ever understood the question. He was like you in that respect."

The compliment made Jake ill at ease. "You put me in lofty company," he said.

"No. You put yourself there. You're the best—I'm living proof." Gloria stopped at Jake's obvious discomfort. "I don't mean to embarrass you," she said.

"You didn't."

"I did. If I didn't know better, I'd say you're blushing. Why? Why can't you take a compliment?"

"I don't know."

"Yes, you do."

Jake shrugged. "Maybe I do," he said.

"Tell me."

"You're like Mrs. Preston. She praises Oliver; you're thankful I saved your life."

"What's wrong with that?"

"Nothing, except that we invent ourselves and those around us all the time. We cover up the weaknesses of those we're fond of and enhance the weaknesses of those we don't like. Oliver, in Mildreth's memory, is like a god. I'm not. I never will be. I just want to make sure it's the real me you're praising, not some glossy image of me."

Gloria leaned back, hurt. "You're not very tactful, are you?" Jake didn't defend his directness. He'd take a straight line to honesty every time, aware that the bumps in the road were sometimes the feelings of those he cared for.

"What else do you remember about Oliver Preston?" he asked finally.

Gloria was thankful to be on another subject. "He worked as an environmental consultant for The Gorham Corporation for a bit."

"When was this?"

"Twenty years ago, maybe more. He did an environmental audit of our company and came up with plans to make GC more 'earth compatible.' That's Oliver's phrase. Dad was all for it. In fact, he was one of the first in the business world to take Oliver's ideas seriously. They were both visionaries." Gloria's eyes sparkled faintly. "I think Milly's idea for a memorial for Oliver is wonderful. It's simple and natural, just like he was."

"Only not so simple now that Colin Owens has disappeared. I think I'll take a little ride up to Winslow and have a look around. Care to join me?"

"When?"

"As soon as I go back to my place and pack a bag."

Jake knew the answer before she spoke. "I don't think so," she said. "There are a few things I want to do on *Gamecock*."

"You're going to have to rejoin the world sometime. You can't hide in this old wooden boat forever."

Like the sun being shadowed by a passing cloud, her expression darkened grimly. "I know that, Jake," she told him. "But right now, all I can manage is this old boat. Give me time."

"You got it," he said. Leaning across the cockpit, he kissed her. "You sure you're all right?"

"I'm all right," she repeated.

He knew she wasn't, just as he knew there was nothing he could do to make her feel any better. He clapped his hands and Watson jumped to his feet. "Thanks for keeping an eye on Watson while Mrs. Preston looked me over."

She forced a smile. "Anytime."

"I'll let you know where I'm staying."

She nodded, and her eyes followed him as he walked down the dock.

There are no welcoming signs on the two-lane back road that cuts into the steep, tree-lined granite foothills of New Hampshire's Green Mountains. But signs aren't necessary. The roads—narrow, potholed, crowned, and curving past stone walls and twisting cool creeks—announce the arrival of another time and an unfamiliar place.

Jake's Saab banked around the curves, down the looping turns rising and falling with the sudden frost heaves and dips that were often so abrupt they woke Watson, who slept in the back with the seat down. Watson had huge pool eyes, a thick, shiny black coat, and a sturdy snout. He was kind and loyal like all good dogs; what made him different was his ability to spot danger and his willingness—when it involved Jake—to confront it. Jake thought of him as a psychic middleweight fighter.

After another swooping plunge in the road, Watson got up and looked out the back window as Preston Mountain fell out of view. At the foot of the mountain, the road leveled off and followed the Ashuelot River toward the village of Winslow. Large decaying houses sat near the river, barns tilting ready to fall, junk cars cluttering front yards with the reminder that not all villages are kept up for tourists and postcards. Some—such as Winslow—appeared dark, turned back on themselves, totally unfamiliar with the expectations of travelers. Winslow was an open, festering wound.

What was it that Mildreth Gibbon Preston had told Jake about Winslow? It was the closest village to her property, it had an inn where Jake could stay, and the people weren't ashamed of their hard lives. As Jake slowed down for the turnoff to the Inn at River

Bend, he wondered if the disappearance of Colin Owens could somehow be tied to a village that looked as though it was about to fall in on itself.

He downshifted into third, wheeled into the inn's gravel parking lot, and shut off the engine. The Inn at River Bend was a sprawling, irregularly shaped, red-painted Federal-style building with chimneys at each end, a wraparound front porch overlooking the river, and six-over-six windows with a small electrified candle in each. Jake thought that the inn, at night with the candles lit, must look like an old-world mansion rising above what was otherwise a small, unremarkable village. According to Mildreth Preston, during the day and early evening, the inn was the focus of social contact. Breakfast, lunch, and dinner were served seven days a week in the small combination dining room and bar to passers-by and residents alike who had neither the interest nor energy to drive another twenty miles to the restaurants in Keene.

Jake climbed the porch steps and opened the front door. The interior was dimly lit with cheaply stained wainscoting, wallpaper curling at the edges, and water stains on the ceiling.

Could use a wrecking ball, Jake thought as he took the pen from the desk and signed in.

"Can I help you?" asked Daniel Dodge as he came down the stairs carrying a water pitcher and a tray of empty glasses. He was tall, somewhere past early retirement, with thin wisps of white hair and round wire-rimmed glasses.

"You must be Jake Eaton," he said, putting down the tray and stepping behind the counter. Jake shook his outstretched hand. "We don't have many guests midweek. Not that we have many weekends either, but welcome all the same."

"Thank you."

"Be staying long?"

"For a few days anyway," Jake said as Watson strolled onto the porch and sat, having taken a little run about the place. Jake opened the door and let him in.

"That the dog you mentioned over the phone?" Dodge asked with a kindly smile. "Be an extra three dollars a night, like I said."

"His name's Watson."

"Friendly?"

"Most of the time."

"I'll tell Lottie Ruggles that. She cleans the rooms," the innkeeper said, finishing the registration card and handing a room key to Jake. "Top of the stairs, left side. Nice view of the river. Most folks like it. I'm sure you will too."

"Colin Owens hasn't steered me wrong yet," Jake said and watched a quizzical look furrow Dodge's brow.

"Don't believe I know the man."

"No? I was sure Colin recommended you." Jake fished a little deeper. "He was up here two weeks ago or so doing some aerial surveying."

"Ahhh," Dodge said abruptly. "That's the fella who's missing. I knew I'd heard the name, but he didn't stay here. No, sir. Don't know where he stayed, but check it out with Sheriff Sellers. He knows every step taken in the village."

"Where might I find him?" Jake asked.

"Hard to say, but it can't be far in a village this size. He'll turn up in a couple of hours." The innkeeper smiled sociably. "Come up from Boston way, did you?"

Jake nodded.

"How was the traffic?"

"Didn't slow down until I hit the mountains."

Dodge nodded agreement. "The big one does take a while to climb over," he said. "It's named for our village eccentric."

"And who might that be?"

"The lady the mountain's named after—Milly Preston. Only she doesn't live here."

"No?"

Dodge shook his head. "Never did, but she might as well have as much as folks talked about her and Oliver. I mean, what kind of man is smart enough to win a Nobel Prize and dumb enough to buy a mountain he never put a ski run on?"

"Your sentiments?" Jake asked as Dodge folded his arms against his chest and shook his head.

"No, sir. Not mine. I never met either one of them. I'm just telling you what I've heard. I'm a retired insurance man, Mr. Eaton.

When my wife died, I left New Jersey looking for someplace as far
away from bad air and rush hour traffic as I could get. I found it
right here."

"How long have you been in Winslow?"

"Five years. Some folks use my first name now. That's just the
way I like it. Slow change or no change is fine with me," he said
and went back to work.

Jake picked up his bag and climbed the stairs with Watson at
his side.

The room was comfortably furnished with a maple four-poster
bed, a pine writing desk with a brass student lamp, a pine cottage
chest, a wing chair, and an oval braided rug covering the uneven,
wide pine floorboards. Being a corner room, there was plenty of
light and good views of the river out the front and the mountains
to the side. Jake unpacked his change of clothes, filled Watson's
food and water bowls, then checked the load of his .38-caliber
Smith & Wesson before putting it back in his shoulder holster. He
caught a glimpse of himself in the full-length mirror that hung
inside the closet door.

He'd run track in college and hadn't yet lost the muscular lean-
ness he carried well on his six-foot frame. True, the brown hair
was thinning and the square face was not as honest as it once was
after years of listening to clients' accusations and resentments, but
Jake still passed for interesting looking if not handsome, with
bright, piercing brown eyes and a thick, well-trimmed mustache.
He was a casual dresser, most often wearing chinos, T-shirts or
turtlenecks, running shoes, and a sportcoat cut full enough to
hide his gun. April in New Hampshire required a sweater and a
Gore-Tex shell, which he pulled from his bag and put on. The
loose-fitting shell camouflaged any bulge of the .38.

Jake picked up the phone and dialed Sheriff Sellers's office. After six rings and no answer, he hung up.

—3—

Failing to reach Myron Sellers, Jake drove south to Keene, a sleepy New England town of twenty-two thousand people. He wanted to talk to Lieutenant Moreau, the man Mildreth Preston had told him was in charge of finding Colin Owens. He left Watson in the car in the shade of a building and walked into the Keene Police Department.

Jake stopped at the door with the lieutenant's name on it, knocked, and entered. "I'm looking for Larry Moreau," Jake announced and took in the office. It reflected a man who was impersonal and disciplined, a man who was simple, direct, and boring.

Moreau looked up from his paperwork. He was thirty-seven years old with short black hair and a slightly soldierly appearance in his blue suit. "You found him," he said. "What can I do for you, Mr. . . . ?"

"Eaton. Jake Eaton. I'm a private detective from Cambridge."

"Out of state."

"Correct."

"Your license is no good up here," Moreau said, staking his territory.

Jake waved him off. "I'm just passing through, Lieutenant. Doing a friend a favor. No more than that."

Moreau was wary. "And which friend is that?"

No point in mentioning Gloria, Jake thought. "Mildreth Gibbon Preston."

17

Moreau motioned Jake to a chair. "So," he said, sighing, "she finally did it. She went private on me." The lieutenant thought a moment, then said, "She think I'm not doing the job 'cause I can't find some fella who got himself lost in the woods?"

"Is that what your investigation points to? Owens is taking a few days off and not telling his wife?"

Moreau acted as if he hadn't heard. His eyes narrowed into slits. "Milly Preston didn't need to send you," he said. "I've already told her we're doing all we can."

"I'm sure you are, Lieutenant," Jake said, trying for Moreau's good side. "I told her the same thing."

"Then what are you doing up here?" Moreau asked stubbornly.

"Like I said, looking around, reporting back. You won't even know I'm here."

"A P.I. not authorized to work in this state—I'd better not."

"I hear you, Lieutenant. All I want to do is enough so I can look my friend in the eye and tell her the truth."

"And that is?"

"Like you said, you've got everything under control."

Moreau looked as though knew he was being massaged but said nothing.

"Mind telling me what you've got?" Jake asked.

Inwardly, the lieutenant minded a great deal but didn't say so. "It's all right here," he said, holding a manila folder in his right hand, not offering it.

"May I?"

Moreau hesitated, then handed it over. Inside was a neatly typed missing-persons report with all the blanks filled. According to what Moreau had written, Colin Owens was a fifty-six-year-old, blue-eyed male with a fair complexion and light brown hair, weighing two hundred pounds at just over six feet. His wife reported him missing thirteen days ago when he failed to return home from a flyover near Winslow, New Hampshire. The line beginning "Places Where He Might Be" listed his home in Medford, his office in Boston, and his summer home on Sebago Lake in Maine.

"He seems to have done all right for himself," Jake said.

"Not bad."

Jake closed the folder and put it back on the desk. "Anybody report seeing him?" he asked.

"We've had a few sightings—all of them right after his picture appeared on the television news. All were checked out; all came up zero. You know how it is—people see something on TV and think they're a part of it. They pick up the phone, give us an inside tip, and off we go on another wild goose chase. The truth is, Colin Owens hasn't been seen anywhere."

"Who saw him last?" Jake asked.

"Folks at the airport." Moreau checked his notes. "Owens signed the plane in at three-thirty in the afternoon, paid his bill, and left the airport—alone—just after four. Three people saw him, and all three swear it was no later than four-fifteen when he left."

"Any idea where he was going?"

"I know exactly where he went," Moreau said, looking satisfied that he could answer. "He drove north toward Winslow and Mrs. Preston's property. How much do you know about aerial surveys?"

"Not much."

"It's a simple business, really. The pilot flies LAT-LONG coordinates and photographs the property. He makes his passes and shoots the film. But no matter how good he is—and Owens was good—he still has to go back on foot and check out the rocky overhangs, shadowy areas, a stand of evergreens—anything that blocks out a clear view of the boundaries. The way Owens normally worked, he would develop the film, identify the poorly sighted areas, and send a crew up for another look. Since he didn't this time, my guess is he spotted something interesting from the air and went back to check it out himself. That's when he ran into Myron Sellers."

"The part-time sheriff in Winslow."

Moreau shook his head disapprovingly. "So, you *have* been doing a little investigating."

"Mildreth Preston filled me in before I drove up. Was Sellers the last person to see Owens?"

"As far as I can tell. Myron saw Owens's car parked on the Preston land and checked it out."

"Did he *see* Owens?"

"He did. Owens had come down the mountain and was getting in his car. According to Myron, they didn't have much of a conversation. 'Nice day'—things like that."

Jake leaned back in his chair, disappointed. "I'd like to talk to Sellers, if you don't mind."

"I don't mind, but it won't do you much good," Moreau said. He leaned forward on his desk, his hands clasped, lecture style. "You have to understand New Hampshire to appreciate this, but we've got hundreds of tiny villages that have a police officer only because it lowers their municipal insurance rate. Most folks who run and get elected understand that. They know they're supposed to stay out of the way and let us career officers handle any trouble. Only Myron never went along with that. He took his election for real and pokes his big nose into everything—mostly at the wrong time. This time, however, he may have been of help. He swears that Owens was just coming back to his car, happy as could be."

"Only, he never made it home." Jake reminded him.

"That's right. He never did. Neither his car nor Colin have been seen since."

"How about credit cards? Gas charges? Anything that might provide a lead?"

Moreau shook his head. "It's like he stepped off the end of the world."

"Even that takes money."

"Which is another thing. His wife said he didn't have much on him. Two, three hundred maybe. There was nothing out of the ordinary to indicate he was thinking about taking off. From what I can gather, Terry and Colin Owens had it pretty good."

"You've talked to her?"

"Two or three times. There's no skeleton in the closet that I can see. The guy's got a nice wife, three nice kids, a nice home, and a successful business. What's he want to take off for?"

"Maybe he didn't."

"Enemies?"

"We've all got a few."

Moreau reached behind him and pulled the sheet of paper

from the typewriter. Across the top of the page was the all-capped heading: "SUSPECTS/MOTIVES/MISSING PERSON: COLIN OWENS."

"I was just finishing this up when you came in." Moreau turned the page for Jake to see. Other than the headline, it was blank. "I come up with nothing. The man had no enemies."

"So where is he?" Jake asked.

Moreau shook his head. "Don't know. All I know is the guy's got a happy marriage. He and his wife are active in their church, they're social drinkers, neither runs around except when Terry gets a hit on the PTA softball team. She plays second base; Colin coaches and brings the beer cooler. She loves the man."

"Maybe he doesn't love her," Jake offered.

"So he runs off?"

"It happens."

"Not this time." Moreau leaned back in his chair and clasped his hands behind his head. "No way, no sir, I'm not buying it."

"What are you buying, Lieutenant?"

Moreau released his hands and once again leaned forward on his desk. "I'm not far enough along in my investigation to be able to answer that," he said, making sure Jake understood who was in charge. "You might tell Mrs. Preston that the next time you see her. How soon will that be?" Moreau wanted to know.

"Meaning when am I going back?"

"Precisely. When are you going back?"

Jake shrugged. "Thought I might take a day or so to relax up here in the mountains."

"Uh-huh."

"Nothing official."

"No. Just helping out your friend."

"That's right, Lieutenant." Jake stood. "One thing. How'd Owens spend his free time?"

"Flying."

"Wouldn't that be work?"

"Not for him. That's how the guy let his hair down. He took off in an airplane every chance he got. Even had model planes in his office and pictures of them on the walls. I checked his records over the past six months, and he was in the air more than he was on the ground."

"Was that unusual?"

"Not so you'd notice. He was the best. I guess that's why Mrs. Preston hired him." Moreau paused and let a cool gaze settle on Jake. "Too bad she doesn't hold me in such high regard."

"It's not regard, Lieutenant. It's just that she doesn't like being ignored."

"What's that supposed to mean?"

"It means when she calls, you should talk to her."

"As if I've got nothing else to do."

Jake walked toward the door. "And talk nice. She's from the old school."

"I know where she's from."

Jake stopped at the door and turned to face Moreau. "I'm at the Inn at River Bend. I'll be there for a couple of days."

"Yeah, sure. Just relaxing."

Jake smiled. "That's right, Lieutenant. Mind telling me how to get to the airport?"

Moreau's expression turned skeptical. "Going somewhere?" he asked.

"To look at some planes."

—4—

The mountains surrounding the small private airport just outside of Keene made taking flying lessons there a dicey proposition unless the plane had good brakes and the pilot was skilled in short landings. Still, Jason Malone, the stocky, solid-looking owner-operator, told Jake he'd never lost a plane or a pilot.

"Until now," he added, shaking his head in disbelief. "I don't believe Colin ran off—not for a minute."

"How well did you know him?" Jake asked as they walked toward the four-seat Cessna that Owens had chartered for his flyovers. Watson, his eyes blinking and watering at the low afternoon sun, stayed close to Jake's side.

"Well enough, I guess. I chartered him planes for ten years, drank a few beers with him when he didn't have to rush off. Always in a rush, Colin was. Always."

They stopped on the closely cropped grass behind a metal hangar where the single-engine light gray plane sat tethered to eyebolts buried in cement and sunk deep in the ground. The warm sun reflected off the propeller blades.

"This is it," Malone said and opened the flimsy door. "Nothing much to doing a survey. The camera's mounted inside with the lens directed down through that opening there on the undercarriage. The pilot flies over the site and clicks away. It's just like shooting baby pictures without waiting for the smile."

"How much time does it take?"

"Once he's over the site, it depends on the size of the area he's got to cover. One eight-by-ten photo covers three hundred acres, tops. But it all depends on the terrain. If he can't see the ground control points, he's got to come in lower and maybe shoot only two hundred acres a print."

"How long was Colin gone?" Jake asked.

"The first flyover, he was gone six hours. The second, he went up and back in three, maybe four hours. I'd have to check the records to be sure, but something like that. With twenty thousand acres, guys not as experienced as Colin might take three, maybe four trips to get it all," Malone said, shutting the cockpit door while Watson darted off after a startled field mouse.

"Do you charter this plane to anyone other than Owens?"

"To anyone with a pilot's license and five hundred dollars, but Colin was my best customer." Malone removed his cap and ran his hand through his brown hair. "Fact is, I always figured Colin would buy another plane of his own," he said, tugging his cap back on.

"He used to own one?"

"Years back, yeah. An earlier model of what he charters from me. She was a real honey. Too bad he had to get rid of it," Malone said. "It tore him up being without a plane. Tore him up real bad."

"How'd he come to lose it?"

"The way you lose anything: money trouble. When he first started surveying, business was down, nobody was buying houses, nobody was building houses, nobody needed a surveyor. But Colin still had a mortgage, a family, another baby on the way, and no bucks. He'd fly for anybody just to keep his head above water, but there weren't many takers. Pretty soon, the bank took his plane. But it worked out for the best, I guess."

"How so?" Jake asked as Watson tired of playing with the mouse and trotted back to his side.

Malone shrugged. "I don't know. It just seemed like not long after, he was rolling in some good money. Colin had a thing about being strapped for cash. He hated being without. I guess that's why he's always carried a lot on him."

Jake looked at Malone quizzically. "According to Lieutenant

Moreau, Colin's wife said he came up here with two, maybe three hundred dollars."

"Just goes to show you what wives know," Malone said with a grin. "Not that I tell mine everything either—hell, no. Be a dull life without airplanes and women."

"Owens played around?"

Malone looked uncomfortable. "Come on, man," he said. "This can't be important."

"Might be," Jake said. "What was Owens mixed up in?"

Malone's attention went out toward the runway. Finally, he cut Jake a look as if the answer were obvious. "He gambled. He played cards, big time."

"How big?"

"More than you and I could afford to lose. I've seen him lay down thousands." Malone flashed his impish smile. "To snap pictures from an airplane, you've got to have crystal clear weather. No fog, no low clouds, no nothing that might ruin the shot. When you don't have it, you can stand around and spit like a baseball player or you can play cards and wait for the weather to break."

"Did he play here?"

Malone stiffened. "No comment."

Jake's expression soured. "You're wasting my time," he said. "Talk to me."

"Look," Malone offered. "If this gets back to Lieutenant Moreau, he'd shut me down in a minute."

"I'm listening."

Ill at ease, Malone kicked at the dirt. "Myron Sellers was one of our regulars, too," he let out. "Myron was going to tip me off if Moreau ever got wise. Myron was like that. He'd give you a break."

"And Moreau wouldn't?"

"Moreau's by the book. Everything's on the table."

"And Sellers—is what—under it looking for a handout?"

"No way, man. He didn't need handouts," he said, shaking his head vigorously. "Myron won damn near every time he pulled up a chair, especially when Colin was playing. I tell you, Myron prayed for rain when he knew Colin had a charter. It was like he could look right into that man's eyes and see what cards he held in his hand. Colin never won a pot. Least it seemed that way."

"Did a lot of people know he was flying the Preston survey?" Jake asked.

"The memorial for Oliver Preston made all the papers, but I don't think anybody knew Colin was doing the flyover. What difference would it make?"

"It'd be an easy way to set up a robbery if you knew a man carrying a few thousand was going to be at the airport," Jake said, thinking of Winslow and some of the run-down houses he'd seen there. In general, New Hampshire was not a wealthy state. "I'd like the names of all the men Colin played cards with," Jake added.

"Come on, man!" Malone protested. "Those guys are friends of mine. If I'd wanted that information out, I would've come clean with the lieutenant."

"You should have," Jake told him. "Makes it easier for all of us to find Colin Owens. You do want him found?"

"Of course." Malone's voice had lost its steam. He looked warily at Jake. "Why do you ask that?"

"You lied to the lieutenant. No reason you aren't lying to me."

"I'm not lying, all right? I want Colin found as much as the next guy."

"Then you'll get me the names."

Reluctantly, Malone answered. "Yeah, I'll get you the names. But they won't be of any help."

"We'll see," Jake said. Then he added, "Just in case you decide to hold out on me, I'm going to ask Sellers to provide his own list. Tap into his sense of civic duty."

"He doesn't have any," Malone spit out.

"Just as long as you do," Jake said and walked along with Watson toward his car.

It was late afternoon when Jake pulled in front of the one-story red clapboard building, got out of his car, and climbed the front wooden stairs. "Town Office, Winslow, N.H., Open M-W-F, 9 to Noon" was painted on the door to the left, "Sheriff Myron Sellers, M–F, Noon to 3" was painted on the door to the right. Jake knocked on the sheriff's side and got no answer. The town side was also closed and empty, the shades drawn.

He was about to leave when Watson, his back bristling, dug at the door with a whine.

"What is it, boy?"

The hairs along Watson's spine stood up straight as he let out a growl that rumbled from deep in his throat.

Jake cupped his hands to shade his eyes against the sun's reflection and peered through the small crack not covered by the drawn window shade. He could see nothing, but he trusted Watson's intuition. He drew his .38 and nudged the door with his foot. It was unlocked and opened onto a scene from a B movie: books were torn from the shelves, file cabinets were ripped open, manila folders and police reports were scattered across the desk and floor. The gun cabinet was smashed and broken into, and the back door was slightly ajar. There was no sign of Myron Sellers, but Jake knew as surely as if he'd been carrying a Geiger counter that he was not alone.

Jake picked his way through the mess with short, careful steps. Watson moved ahead in a crouch, his anvil-shaped head swinging left and right with each slow stride until he stopped at a closet door. It was the only place anyone could hide.

Jake moved quickly past the dog to the back door. He pushed against it with his shoulder, staying clear of any possible prints on the knob. The door opened fully, and Jake stepped outside, his gun ready. No one was in sight.

He came back inside, his attention now focused on the closet. He readied his .38 and said in a firm voice, "When I open the door, I want to see your hands on your head. Ready?" He waited briefly, then jerked the closet door open. Into his outstretched arms fell a heavyset man with thinnish red hair.

Jake caught him and gently laid him down. He holstered his revolver, then felt for a pulse. The man was dead.

A small-caliber entry wound still trickled blood. He hadn't been dead long. Jake started with the left front shirt pocket and searched the body. He came up empty. He rolled the body over, pulled out the wallet, opened it, and extracted the driver's license.

The mug shot matched that of Myron Sellers, now deceased. He put the license back and opened the money slot. Jake took out the money and counted two thousand dollars, mostly in one-hundred-dollar bills. Not bad for a part-time sheriff, Jake thought as he put back the money.

He stood and stepped away from the body. He knew cops who could enter a crime scene and immediately put themselves into the mind of the killer. On occasion that assuredness swept through him, and he could relive the crime step by step as if playing it back on videotape. However, standing next to Sellers, looking down at the blank eyes, he could only feel the fat man's surprise and pain—the overwhelming horror he must have experienced knowing that someone was about to kill him.

Jake walked to Sellers's desk and put in a call to the Keene police. In the half an hour it took for Lieutenant Moreau and the state police forensics team to arrive, Jake searched the office, going back to the sheriff once to close his eyes.

—5—

The crime-scene photographer was inside Sellers's office snapping pictures while the medical examiner looked over the body and pronounced the sheriff dead. Their actions were routine and swift. Larry Moreau, on the other hand, moved as if in slow motion, apparently overwhelmed by the chaos of the office and the distinct smell of death.

Jake stood near the front door. Outside, the curious were lined up against the yellow police tape as if waiting to buy tickets. The one constant in every catastrophe was the onlookers who wanted a peek at the less fortunate.

"You ever notice that, Lieutenant?" Jake asked.

Moreau looked up from his own personal daze. "Notice what?" he asked, the uncertainty heavy in his voice.

"How other's misfortunes are like a magnet. People can't stay away."

Moreau rubbed the back of his neck as he turnd to the young officer next to him. "You done with that statement yet?" he asked grumpily.

"Just finishing up, Lieutenant," Officer Slocum said, pencil on his pad, Jake's final answer noted. John Slocum was a weed of a man, a boy really, Jake thought, with long, spidery features and sloping, undeveloped shoulders. Jake guessed that for Slocum as well as Moreau, this was their first murder investigation.

"Get all you can, then get him the hell out of here," Moreau ordered.

"I've got it all, sir," Slocum answered.

"Then you know what to do, don't you, Eaton?" Moreau was struggling as if no solid ground were beneath his feet.

Jake nodded, embarrassed for the man before him. "I know what to do, Lieutenant. I'll be around if you need me."

"Don't count on it," Moreau said, saving face.

"No," Jake told him. "Wouldn't ever count on it."

Moreau cut Jake an appreciative glance, then Jake headed for his car. It was a long drive to the Owens's house.

Terry Owens was sitting across from Jake in the living room, staring at her cigarette, nervously waiting for him to tell her that the calamity caused by her missing husband was over. It had all been a mistake, a wrinkle in the cosmos, stars orbiting too close to one another. Something. Anything but this itchy silence. Finally, she broke it.

"I spoke to Mrs. Preston last night. She said you'd left for Winslow."

"I did."

"Back so soon?" She was gaunt and weary. Jake couldn't tell if she was forty-five or fifty-five, but her eyes—bloodshot and with a vacant stare—made her seem worn thin regardless of her age. "I mean, back with good news, I hope."

Jake felt sorry for her. He'd knocked unannounced on her door at nine o'clock at night. He hadn't brought good news; he'd brought news that the last person to see her husband lay dead in his office. He felt the way a pilot must feel just before he drops a bomb on an unsuspecting civilian. Jake decided not to drop it, not yet.

"Why didn't you tell the police that your husband was a compulsive gambler?" he asked.

The smoky veil made Mrs. Owens look fragile and untouchable. "Was. Past tense." Her voice was a long way away.

In the corner, one of her three daughters giggled and tugged Watson's ears. Watson held his own under the playful assault.

"That part of our lives is over," she said, taking the last draw on her cigarette. She rubbed it out in the ashtray beside her on the glass-topped table. "There's little about those years I like to re-member. Colin had no control of himself; he finally came to be-lieve it when he had to sell his airplane to cover his debts. Back then," she said evenly, "he loved the roll of the dice and flying more than me or the children. He never believed he could lose. The fact was he seldom won." She lit another cigarette, filled her lungs with smoke, and looked down at her lap as the smoke rolled.

Then she looked up at Jake. "We were living in Framingham with two children in one of those horrible red brick apartment buildings that people never get out of. I knew we were never go-ing to get out of there. Colin never saved any money. It was im-possible for him. It'd hit his pocket and be gone. Vanish, just like his airplane. Right after the bank repossessed the plane, I took the children and left him."

"When was this?" Jake asked.

"Fifteen years ago, a little more, maybe. We've been married twenty-three. These last years have been wonderful, really. Colin promised to get help, to straighten himself out, and I gave him another chance. We sort of started over when we moved here," she said, looking over at her children climbing on the docile dog. "We even decided to have a third child. I don't believe he'd throw it all away again. There must be some mistake. I know he wouldn't throw it all away."

"Did your husband ever mention Myron Sellers?"

"No." She thought a moment. "No, I don't think so. Who is he?"

"The sheriff in Winslow and the last man to see your husband after he left the airport. He and Colin played a few hands of poker now and again."

Terry Owens glared at her cigarette. Jake leaned back in his chair. "They got to be friendly," he said. "Friendly enough for Sell-ers to recommend your husband to Mrs. Preston. Strange that Colin never mentioned him."

"My husband is an excellent surveyor," she said defensively. "He knows hundreds of people I don't."

"Then, there's the matter of the money," Jake said, studying her as if her expression, not her answers, held the truth. "You say your husband left here with only a few hundred dollars."

"I ought to know. I do all the bookkeeping."

"Do you know Jason Malone?"

"By name only. I've never met him, but I've made out checks to his airport."

"According to Malone, your husband always carried big money. Always," Jake said as her face went flat. "Where'd he get it, if you didn't give it to him?"

"I don't know."

"A business account, maybe?"

"I already told you, I handle the money for the business and the house. Colin left here with a few hundred dollars, no more. He went up to Winslow to fly a survey. He got up in the morning like any other husband; he hugged his children like any other husband and went off to work like any other husband and . . . and . . . you come into his house and accuse him . . ." Her body trembled and her hand shook.

Jake leaned toward her. "Mrs. Owens, I know this is a hard time for you, but—"

"No buts," she snapped. "He made a fool out of me once with a thousand stories about where the money went. 'Gambling? No, never.' And I came back, and together we've built a good life. But if he's made a fool out of me this time . . . if he's made a fool of me by abusing the kindness of Mildreth Preston . . . if he's gambling again, I don't want him back." She jammed her cigarette into the ashtray and stood.

The children stopped playing and looked at her. "It's all right," she said to them, but even she didn't seem to believe it. Nothing seemed right since Colin disappeared. She retook her seat and folded her hands together. She looked hard at Jake. "I do not believe one word you're saying to me, Mr. Eaton. My husband is the victim here, not the other way around. If you've heard he's gambling, you've heard people lying. I don't know why, but that's what it is—lies, nothing more. All I know is that something has happened to my husband, and for some reason people in that village are not telling you the truth. If I were you, I'd drive back to Winslow and start with the sheriff. Ask him why he's spreading lies about Colin playing a few hands of cards."

Jake dropped the bomb. "The sheriff's dead," he told her, watching her expression slacken to shock.

"How?"

"Shot."

"Dear God."

She didn't move, she couldn't. She was in that emotional no-man's-land, disarmed and vulnerable.

Jake felt a pang of sympathy. He'd dragged the poor woman into an emotional rathole; he'd help get her out. He stood and walked to the kitchen. A bottle of scotch was on the counter. Two glasses were washed and dried next to it. Curious, Jake thought, pouring a glass and taking it to her. She drank, her eyes glassy and distant. Jake sat across from her.

"I need your help, Mrs. Owens. Winslow is a small village. It would be one hell of a coincidence if your husband's disappearance and Sellers's death weren't related."

"I don't know anything about it." She was rocking back and forth, hunched over at the waist.

"Mrs. Owens . . ."

"I don't. I don't know anything about it." She glared at Jake and began to cry uncontrollably.

Jake stayed with Terry Owens until she stopped trembling, then got in his car and headed down Route 16 for home. At the rotary, he swung left onto Alewife Brook Parkway. The late-night traffic had thinned out even past the Cambridge malls, making the late-model tan Ford following him easy to spot. It had two men in the front seat.

"Company," Jake mumbled to Watson. "Shall we find out who they are?"

Watson cocked his head.

"I think so, too," Jake said, slowing to a Sunday-afternoon, look-at-the-roses pace.

The Ford followed, making the turn on Linnenan a block after Jake made it. Jake turned left on Avon and parked in the first space he found. He pulled his .38 and rolled the driver's-side window all the way down.

The Ford slowed at the intersection, turned in, then backed out and headed off in the direction it had come. Jake waited twenty minutes for them to circle the block. When they didn't, he locked his Saab and walked to Martin Street and his combination office-condo.

Jake and Watson walked the four flights of stairs to the top floor and entered. The office part of the four-room apartment was decorated with a Sheraton-style mahogany double desk, red leather club chair and ottoman, brass floor lamps, and Oriental rugs. Across the hall was the eat-in kitchen with an enormous white porcelain sink on legs that Jake would have replaced with a cabinet had this not been one of Watson's favorite sleeping spots. Down the hall to the left was the living room; one end was lined with mahogany glass-doored bookcases. A writing desk stood along one wall. Opposite it, a greenish gray brocade sofa sat beneath two street-facing windows. The bedroom and bath were down the hall to the right.

Jake made himself a vodka gimlet and freshened Watson's food and water. They both drank, then Jake asked his partner, "Any ideas who'd want to tail us?"

Watson shifted from water to food.

"Me neither," Jake said and followed Watson's lead. He was about to decide which take-out sounded better—pepperoni pizza from Harvard House, or beef gingers with spicy tofu from Thai Cuisine—when the phone rang.

Jake picked it up.

"Mr. Eaton." It was a woman's voice he hadn't expected. "Thank God you're home. I didn't want to leave such a horrible message on your machine. Myron Sellers has been killed. That lieutenant . . . oh, what is his name?"

"Moreau."

"Yes." Mildreth Preston paused to catch her breath. "Moreau. I . . . I'm not thinking too clearly at the moment. Let me collect my thoughts and then . . . oh, yes. Lieutenant Moreau. He called me with the terrible news that Myron had been shot."

"I know," Jake told her. "I found the body."

"And you didn't see fit to tell me?" Her voice fluttered indignantly.

"I phoned the police, then drove back to see Terry Owens."

"Dear God." Mildreth's voice was full of dread. "That was my worst fear when I heard. Colin Owens's disappearance is somehow connected with Myron Sellers's death, isn't it?"

"It would make sense," Jake said. "Sellers recommended Owens to you. Somehow, you and your property are right in the middle of something."

"Of what?"

"That's what I'm going back to Winslow to find out."

—6—

Long after Mildreth Gibbon Preston had hung up, Jake stood near his desk leaning his head against the wall. His simple favor to Gloria to talk to Milly Preston was closing in around him. He didn't like the feeling. He hadn't wanted Mildreth Preston as a client in the first place, regardless of her five hundred dollars a day. New clients were distractions, and Jake wanted uncluttered time to sift through the uneasy feelings that flitted around his mind like bees. Gloria was the queen bee.

Since Jake's divorce, he hadn't allowed any woman to get close enough to become a permanent part of his life. Even Gloria didn't mean much to him at first, but she was beginning to, and Jake wanted time to think through what he felt for her. With Myron Sellers dead, he didn't have the time. He picked up the phone and dialed.

"Greetings," he said.

The sound of his voice had Gloria smiling. "From the far north?" she asked playfully.

"Not so far," Jake answered. "I'm back at my place."

"What happened?"

"Milly's case got a little complicated."

"I thought you said there wasn't much to it." Her voice held a hint of suspicion.

"There wasn't. Now, there is."

"What happened?"

"A man's been murdered." Jake sounded like a surgeon explaining an operation.

Gloria gasped, then hesitated. "Colin Owens?"

"No," Jake said and explained about the sheriff.

"I never thought . . . I mean, when I asked you to talk to Milly, I had no idea . . ."

"I know you didn't."

"But a man's been shot." There was a long, difficult silence. "I'm sorry I got you involved with this, Jake."

"I'll take care of it," he told her and gave her his phone number at the inn. "I can't do any more down here, so I'm going back to Winslow."

"Tonight? This late?"

He waited for an invitation to her place. Disappointed he didn't get one, he replied, "It's one of the perks of being a detective—I don't punch a clock. Which means you can call me anytime."

"I know."

"If you need anything . . ."

"I'll call, Jake. I will."

"Promise?"

"Promise."

Jake hoped so and hung up. He found the Owens's number and dialed. Terry Owens answered with a voice as thin as the wire it traveled on.

Jake explained about the two men in the tan Ford who'd followed him from her house to his apartment. "Do you know anyone who drives a car like that?" he asked her.

"No."

"Maybe you've seen it parked nearby?"

"One car is like any other," she said offhandedly.

"Not this one," Jake told her and described the men as best he could. "Do they sound familiar?"

"I told you," she said. "I don't recognize the car and I don't recognize the men. I don't know what you want me to say."

"Just tell the truth, Mrs. Owens. That tail was on me as soon as I left your house. It didn't follow me there."

"You can't be sure of that," she protested.

"It's my job to be sure."

"I'm sorry," she said. "I don't know what to tell you."

"You could tell me about the two glasses."

"What two glasses?"

Jake heard the apprehension in her voice. "The two beside the bottle of scotch in your kitchen," he said. "I thought you might have been expecting company. Two men maybe? Instead, I show up. When I leave, they tag along."

"I don't know what you're talking about."

"Mrs. Owens—"

"Please! Please, leave me alone." She slammed down the phone.

Jake went to the window and looked out. The Ford wasn't there, but he knew as certainly as he knew that Terry Owens was lying that he'd see that car again.

Dinner turned out to be road food at Johnson's Drive-In just off Route 119 on the way to Winslow. It was not what Jake preferred, but he was sure that Myron Sellers would say the same about his condition. Watson, however, loved to ride and eat. He'd stand on the front seat, front paws pressed against the dashboard, waiting for a bump in the road to serve him. If that failed, he was there anticipating the last bite Jake always handed over.

It was past midnight when Jake and Watson walked into the Inn at River Bend and overheard Able Singer trying to come to grips with the world's spin. Able—a medium-weight man with a cheerful outlook and constant smile—was the village optimist to some, the village idiot to others. Regardless, Able was always willing to knock back a few while searching for the silver lining. It was clear to Jake, after he'd ordered a draft and slid into a booth to enjoy it, that tonight, Able was having a hard time finding any lining at all.

"I'm tellin' ya, Danny. I'm tellin' ya . . . You listenin'?" Able asked.

"Of course, I'm listening," Danny Dodge said mechanically as he dried a glass. He'd been listening all night. Able and, it seemed, most of the village had been in with their assessment of who killed the sheriff, making it a good night for business and a bad night for clear thinking. Five years as an innkeeper had taught Dodge that after a few drinks, people would say anything.

"Long as yore listenin'." Able paused, then dug the depths. "It's like I was tellin' ya, it don't make no sense. None a'tall, falla me?"

"I follow you, Able. Absolutely."

Able took another sip of his drink. "Okay, so where's that put us?"

"Right back where we were hours ago," Dodge said unkindly, another glass washed and dried.

"Why'd somebody go an' shoot Myron?"

Danny put away the glass, half listening to his own answers and Able's questions. "I have no idea."

"Me neither, but that sergeant . . . what's his name? Little runt of a guy . . ."

"Moreau."

"That's the one."

"Only he's a lieutenant, Able," Dodge reminded him.

Jake drank half of his beer and listened to the two men wrangle.

"Lieutenant, then." Able was testy. "Whatever the hell he is, walkin' around here like a banty rooster askin' if anybody'd seen anything. Over an' over an' over an' over the same damn questions. Why didn't he use a bullhorn out inna street? Huh, Danny? Answer me that. *Then* tell me why anybody'd wanna shoot Myron."

"I haven't the faintest, Able." Dodge sounded annoyed.

"Nothin' ever happens here, then one day, bango! It starts out like all the rest, but don't you believe it!" Able shook his drunken head. "Myron otta be sittin' right here cussin' spray paint in the hands of the morally depraved. Haulin' in vandals an' the like, throwin' their asses in jail. But, no. The man ends up shot through the head. How come days end up like this? Answer me that."

Dodge shrugged. "Why don't cows fly?" he mumbled to himself.

Able's brows arched. "What's that got ta do with anything? Jesus, Danny! I'm tryin' ta work this out here an' yore goin' off 'bout some damn animal."

"Sorry," Dodge said sheepishly. "Want another?"

"Sure."

"How about you, Mr. Eaton?"

"Please," Jake said, stepping to the bar. "And a beef jerky."

Dodge removed the lid from a large glass jar and held it while

Jake selected a piece of dried beef and handed it over to the anxiously waiting dog. Watson's eyes glowed at the treat.

"Nice dog," Able said as he took a piece of jerky for himself. "Thanks."

"Yore the 'tective, ain't ya?" Able asked, his face pinched and waiting.

"Word travels fast," Jake said.

"It don't have ta go far in Winslow. Right, Danny?"

Dodge served the full glasses. "For once, Able, you're right, but how we found out is no secret, Mr. Eaton."

"Jake."

"Jake. The lieutenant was all around here this afternoon."

"Questionin' folks," Able chimed. "Should'a just gone out inna street with a bullhorn. 'Did anybody see anything?' 'Did anybody hear anything?' 'Does anybody have any idea why someone would want ta kill the sheriff?' Over an' over an' over 'til he got tired or some damn thing an' went home."

"Before he left," Dodge said, ignoring the drunk, "the lieutenant mentioned you were working for Milly Preston."

Able tugged at the jerky. "An' he also said you an' him might be workin' t'gether on a murder 'vestigation, you bein' a 'tective an' all," Able said as if he didn't believe it. Jake did look more like a college professor than a private cop.

Jake wasn't amused. He tossed Watson another jerky. "I've already got a partner."

"Don't matter. You could have a whole army an' it wouldn't matter one bit." Able was in full grin. "Even a private 'tective can't arrest a ghost."

"That's enough, Able," Dodge cautioned.

"I can't help it ya don't believe me."

"Not today, Able." Dodge's voice was a tired warning.

"Think it might scare off the 'tective?"

"I think you might make a fool of yourself is what I think."

"Yore too damn touchy, Dan," Able protested.

"And you're drunk."

"The hell."

"Good night, Able."

"No it ain't."

"See you tomorrow, Able."

"You tryin' ta run me off?" Able stiffened on the bar stool.

"First one tomorrow's on me," Dodge coaxed.

"If I come back. May not."

Able was off the stool and wobbling. The sound of the front door slamming brought a prim woman in her early sixties out of the kitchen where she'd been cleaning. Before she uttered a word, Jake sensed an unhappiness about her that made her tight and tense. When she saw Mr. Dodge, she said apologetically, "I thought maybe it was Kenney coming in."

"Out late again?" Dodge asked, then corrected his manners. "Lottie," he said, "I don't believe you've met our new guest. Jake Eaton and his dog . . ."

"Watson," Jake added. "He's friendly."

Lottie stood rod straight, ignoring Jake and the dog. Her face was expressionless.

"It was just Able," Dodge said as Lottie turned back toward the kitchen without saying any more. Dodge watched her go. "That was Lottie Ruggles," he finally explained to Jake. "She and her son, Kenney, were living here when I bought the inn. Couldn't run it without them and, frankly, wouldn't want to. They're sort of fixtures in the place." He leaned close to Jake so he could whisper. "John Ruggles—Able's 'ghost'—is Lottie's dead husband."

"What happened?" Jake asked wondering why Lottie was so un-friendly.

"Suicide. It was before my time, but the story goes that he blew his head off right in his own living room. It wasn't much of a place to begin with from what I heard. A run-down worthless dump. The same could be said for Old John himself. A worthless bastard who should've shot himself a thousand times before." Dodge picked up Able's glass and washed it. "Least that's what I heard. The sad part is, with the stories about a suicide floating around, Lottie couldn't sell the house. Before long the bank lost patience and took it away from her. As things go, the fellow I bought the inn from couldn't keep up with the place on his own, so Lottie and her son moved in as sort of caretakers. I was happy they stayed when I bought it. I sure as hell didn't know anything about running an inn. Now I know how to point Able out the door, wipe glasses, and watch Lottie worry herself to death over her boy."

"What's his problem?" Jake asked.

"The problem is he won't listen to his mother."

"Sounds like every kid over the age of twelve."

"Maybe," Dodge consented. "Only Kenney's twenty. And every kid doesn't have a punk like Joey Barns to lead the way down the wrong path. That's where Kenney is tonight. Off again with Joey Barns, looking for trouble."

"What kind of trouble?"

"With Joey, you never know." Dodge reached for Jake's empty glass. "Another?"

"No thanks."

"It's on the house."

Jake shook his head. "I think Watson would like another jerky," he said, pulling one from the jar and handing it to the grateful dog. "Did Sellers have any run-ins with Barns?" Jake asked.

"He did, and I know what you're going to ask next. The answer is 'no.' Joey isn't a murderer. He's a punk."

"Somebody killed Sellers."

"I'm well aware of that."

"So he must've had enemies."

"Sure—every high-school kid who came flying through the village on a Saturday night. Myron was out there waiting for them, ticket pad at the ready. You wouldn't call chasing bored kids police work, but it was about all he had since I've been here. Other than that, he put in a few office hours every day to look professional, then looked for ways to pass the time before driving Able home after I close," Dodge said as Able Singer's slurred voice broke through the night.

"Help! Somebody needs help!" Able shouted. "In the river. Hurry!"

Jake ran out quickly and stopped at the porch. Danny Dodge raced out behind him, Watson at his side. Across the two-lane blacktop at the river's edge stood Able Singer waving frantically toward a yellow kayak.

"Damn fool kid's gonna git hisself drowned," Able shouted over the raging whitewater just as the small boat plowed into a granite jetty.

The half moon was behind the clouds and Jake had trouble seeing anything other than the helmet-covered head jerk violently from side to side in the turbulent rapids. He stepped from the porch and ran to the river's edge.

"Paddle out!" Jake yelled as the boat got caught in an eddy and bounded about like a ball in a pinball machine. "You've got to get away from the rocks. Paddle out!"

"I can't . . . my arm!" The voice was barely audible over the crash and boil of the water that fifteen minutes ago was snow in the mountains.

Dodge took a place beside Able Singer and shouted in Jake's direction. "Boat's gonna flip," he hollered. "Every year somebody underestimates the river. They tire out, and the river takes 'em."

Jake cupped his hands together and yelled toward the bouncing boat. "Can you fend off?"

The kayak crashed into one boulder then glanced off another. The blow sent it downstream fifty yards in seconds. Instinctively, Jake ripped off his jacket and unstrapped his shoulder holster. He was looking for a place to enter the water when Dodge's voice boomed after him.

"You'll last ten minutes in water that temperature. It's running ice. You can't go in there! If the cold doesn't get you, the rocks'll bash you to death."

Jake checked his balance with a swing of his arms. "What's downstream?" he asked.

"Two, three more bad rapids, then she flattens out." Dodge said. "We might catch up to the boat down there."

"If," Able added, "the boat gets through."

"We'll take my car," Jake said, putting on his jacket and picking up his gun. He climbed the riverbank to the blacktop just as a truck engine roared to life about a hundred yards ahead. Jake heard nothing but the untamed water running dark, deep, and cold.

At the top of the hill, the eighteen-wheeler shifted gears and picked up speed. The man in the driver's seat tugged his hat low over his forehead, hunched his shoulders, and with hollow cheeks pulled on his cigarette.

He'd driven this stretch of road hundreds of times. He didn't need headlights, he didn't need anything but the feel of the wheel and the sight of the river on his right.

With precision, he shifted again and eased the accelerator to the floor. The top of the steering wheel was a gun sight, and Jake was zeroed in, motionless, not even looking as the truck barreled down on him.

Watson sensed the danger first and in a shivering instant raced off the porch toward the highway. Jake's attention was downstream on the kayak. To lose sight of it would cost precious minutes, and time was often the deciding factor in life or death.

There was no time to bark a warning when Watson left his feet and flew toward Jake. The truck—a mechanical monster to Watson—would be on his master if he didn't knock him free.

"Look out . . ."

". . . Eaton!"

The warnings were lost in the rush of air as the truck roared by in the moon-sparkled darkness.

Jake was in the breakfast room of the inn working on his second cup of coffee while assessing the aches and pains that had settled in during the night. Besides the bruises, his right eye was swollen nearly shut and a small bandage covered a deep gouge on his forehead. All in all, not too bad for a headfirst dive into some granite boulders. He was beginning to get used to his soreness when the lieutenant stepped to his table.

"You look terrible," Moreau said.

"Good morning to you, too, Lieutenant."

"Mind if I sit?"

"Be my guest," Jake said as Lottie Ruggles and her son—a tall, muscular young man—busily waited tables. The name tag read "Kenney," but "Bored" would have described him better.

Kenney Ruggles sauntered over. "Coffee?" he asked disdainfully.

Moreau answered with a nod. Kenney filled his cup and rattled it across the table to him.

"Refill?" he asked Jake.

"Sure." Jake waited for Kenney to leave. "Must be a joy to have such a son."

"You, too, huh?" Moreau agreed. "I got the same feeling yesterday when I questioned him. I thought it was just because I was a cop." Moreau stirred his coffee, glanced about the room, then looked seriously at Jake's blackened eye. "What happened to you?"

"Someone tried to run me over," Jake said evenly.

Moreau looked startled. "Run you over? When?"

"Last night."

"Did you report it?"

"I didn't report it, Lieutenant. I had a nightcap and went to bed."

"You should've called me."

"You've got enough on your hands. Besides, Watson did just fine. He knocked me out of the way down the riverbank."

Moreau cocked his head. "Who's Watson?" he asked.

"My dog. He looks out for me. I do the same for him."

"Sounds cozy."

"It works."

The lieutenant sipped his coffee, then asked in a hopeful tone, "Any chance it was an accident?"

Jake shook his head. "None. It was a nice little hit-and-run. Somebody put a boat on the river to draw my attention. When they got it, a semi came barreling over the hill."

Moreau shook his head. "I still can't believe it. This is Winslow, for Christ's sake. Stuff like that doesn't happen here."

"*Murder* happened here," Jake reminded him. "Whether you wanted to or not, you've graduated to the big time. When somebody kills a cop, an attempt on my life is a step down."

Moreau didn't like the reprimand, but somewhere inside he felt he deserved it. "Are you suggesting that the same people are involved? Myron's killer made the attempt on you?"

"Killer or killers," Jake said. "Two men have been on my tail since I left Terry Owens's house."

Moreau waited. "And?"

Jake shrugged. "Don't know any more."

"Or you're not telling." Moreau thought a moment. "I'm not a fool, Eaton. Your dog might chase his tail, but I don't spend a lot of time chasing mine."

"Good to know," Jake said, wondering if he'd misjudged the man sitting across from him.

"I think so." Moreau folded his fingers together in front of him. He stared at his hands as he spoke. "Driving up here, I had the thought that I should get you out of my hair. Send you back to Milly Preston with your tail between your legs."

"She wouldn't like that," Jake countered.

"No. But I might. I might like it one hell of a lot. Serve her right if I did."

"Seems like you're fighting the wrong enemy, Lieutenant. You should be after Myron Sellers's killer, not be worrying about me and Mildreth Gibbon Preston."

Moreau glared at Jake. "I haven't forgotten that."

"What do you plan to do about it?"

"What to do with you is the question." Moreau drew his coffee toward him. "I've got an old friend on the Boston PD. I called him when you left my office."

"And?"

"And it seems that messes of this sort are right up your alley."

"People don't call a private detective unless there's a mess."

"True. But I was thinking more about messes we create ourselves. Your brother's death, for example," Moreau said warily, knowing it was a sore subject.

Jake's expression gave no hint that Moreau had hit a nerve. "What about my brother?" he asked coolly.

"Oh, I don't know. You and he were partners, from what I heard."

"That's right."

"Then somebody shot him and beat you almost to death."

"Not 'somebody,'" Jake said, seeing the faces of the men clearly in his mind. He would never forget those faces. "There were two of them," he said. "They shot down my brother like a dog."

Moreau nodded, uncomfortable with the veiled anger in Jake's voice. "My friend said the two guys who did it wound up dead."

"So?"

"So he also said there was some doubt as to who took them out."

Jake's eyes stayed locked on the lieutenant. "There wasn't any doubt," he said calmly.

"There was a rumor you took the law into your own hands."

"I heard that," Jake said.

"Did you?"

"Let's just say justice was done."

"That's not good enough," Moreau said. "I need to know. Did you kill those two men?"

"Boston PD asked that same question."

"And?"

"They let me go, Lieutenant. I kept my license and my gun permit, and I still work with clients like Mildreth Gibbon Preston."

Moreau's troubling thoughts remained. "I don't think I have it in me to kill a man," he admitted.

"Is that why you looked so uncomfortable around Sellers's body?"

"I thought I was going to be sick," he said. He pushed his coffee away and looked up at Jake. "I joined a small-town police force because I wanted to help people. I wanted to be part of a certain way of life."

Norman Rockwell, Jake thought. Barber poles, shady streets, perfect children playing with their perfect puppies. "It's not the place, Lieutenant," Jake said. "It's the times. Every day, Winslow has more in common with New York. You can't escape it. You can only try to slow it down."

"Is that what you do? Try to slow it down?"

"Sometimes."

"And if you don't think you can?"

"I step aside so I don't get run over."

"Only to return more dangerous, like you did with the men who killed your brother."

"I already answered that," Jake said.

"All right. Maybe you'll answer this. Why did you visit Terry Owens?"

"I wanted to ask her about her husband's poker habits."

"Colin was a gambler?"

"So I hear."

"From whom?"

"Jason Malone."

Moreau's expression showed his disappointment. "Malone never told me that." He rubbed his thumb across his knuckles. "So you drove up to the Owens's house?"

"That's right. I got there around nine o'clock."

"And when you left, you were followed?"

"Right again, Lieutenant."

"Any idea who they were?"

"None."

"Guys looking for a time and a place to run you over, maybe?"

Jake shook his head. "I don't think so."

"Why not?"

Jake explained how they didn't take the bait when he parked and waited for them to circle his block. "They're professionals," he told Moreau. "If they wanted to take me out, they had plenty of chances."

"D'you think they hit Sellers?"

"There's one thing I am certain of, Lieutenant. Whoever shot Myron Sellers was anything but a pro."

"You sound damn sure of yourself."

"I am. A professional would have walked in with a twelve-gauge shotgun and blown Sellers in half where they found him. A pro never skimps on firepower and doesn't wince at the sight of blood. He does the job, then forgets about it until the next one comes up. Whoever shot Myron was making it up as he went along."

"What makes you say that?"

"The two thousand dollars in Sellers's wallet."

Moreau scowled. "So," he said, "you did search the body."

"I did. Obviously, the killer didn't. But that raises the more interesting question, Lieutenant. Where'd a part-time sheriff making peanuts get that kind of money?"

"Slocum and I spent the night going through Sellers's office trying to get a lock on that one."

"And?" Jake asked.

Moreau shrugged. "John's the one to talk to. He's going through more stuff as we speak."

"Mind if I talk to him?"

"D'you mean am I going to send you home with your tail between your legs? Not yet," Moreau told him. "Talk to Slocum if you want."

"Thanks," Jake said as Lottie Ruggles set a brown paper bag in front of him.

"Anything else?" she asked, not trying for the friendliness award.

"The check," Jake said, and she put it down.

Moreau looked inside the bag at a plate full of steak and eggs. "Picnic?" he asked.

"A treat," Jake answered and paid the bill. "A little something for Watson for saving my life."

"You're generous," Moreau told him. "You even tip the lady who turned you in as the possible killer."

"Lottie Ruggles saw me go into Sellers's office?"

Moreau nodded. "Saw you go in and come out."

"What was she doing there?" Jake asked.

"That's what I'm here to find out. How about yourself?"

Jake grabbed the bag. "I'm going to feed my dog."

—8—

In back of the inn, a rutted dirt road twisted up a sharp rise, then ended at an abandoned logging road that curved around the hills for miles. In winter, it was a haven for cross-country skiers. In summer with the trees fully leafed, it was like walking in a cavern broken only by flips and charges of strange, eerie light.

Watson—his breakfast eaten—leapt tall grasses as if on springs, his head held high, his eyes darting around and popping wide. A pair of squirrels caught his attention. Watson chased them up tree trunks sending him into fits of frustrated barks until he tired, and walked contentedly alongside Jake.

Jake and Watson followed the path toward the road, crossed the river bridge, and walked up toward Sellers's office. Outside the yellow plastic barrier tape, a dozen or so curious villagers still stood watch, leaning against pickups and whispering. Able Singer was among them. He pointed at Watson and said to the man beside him, "That's the dog right there. Damnedest thing y'ever saw, flyin' through the air like that. I mean it. He musta been ten feet offa the ground."

"Morning," Jake said to Able as he and Watson ducked under the tape.

"Got yer man yet?" Able said with a chuckle.

"Working on it," Jake told him and stepped unannounced into the sheriff's office. Officer Slocum sat behind Sellers's desk logging its contents. The chair seemed to swallow the young officer. All Jake could think of besides the cradle being robbed was that Slocum had barely made the height limit.

Slocum jotted a note on his pad, then looked up. "Didn't you see the tape? Off-limits to all unauthorized personnel." It was a choirboy's voice being forced down an octave.

"Moreau authorized me," he said and introduced himself.

"Oh. Is he over drinking coffee?"

"Something like that," Jake said. "He said you spent the night here."

"Most of it." Slocum looked around at the mess. The thought of logging every item seemed to overwhelm him. "Looks like we might be here another night, too."

Jake nodded agreement. "Pain in the ass."

"Tell me about it," Slocum said, glancing down at Watson sniffing in the corners. "I heard some of the guys say that dog saved your life last night."

"He did."

"Maybe he could help me. Here, boy." The young officer clapped his hands and jumped up from his chair. A startled Watson swerved into some boxes and toppled from them a stack of clumsily piled papers. "It's all right," Slocum explained. "I haven't gotten to those yet."

Jake offered Watson a comforting pat and bent down to collect the papers. A yellowed newspaper in the middle of the pile caught his eye. He pulled it out and looked down on a folded *Boston Globe* dated fifteen years earlier.

"Interesting," he said, opening it carefully. A photograph showed a much younger Oliver Preston standing in a field, arms crossed, piercing eyes looking through his wire-rimmed glasses. Mildreth had similar poses of her husband framed on her mantle. The headline read, "Famous Environmentalist Stops New Hampshire Polluters." Jake waved the clipping toward Slocum. "What's this all about?"

The officer eyed the picture. "Oh, that," he said with a dismissive wave of his hand. "That was nothing."

"It must've been something to Sellers. Otherwise, he'd have pitched the paper." Jake read through the copy. "It says here that Winslow and surrounding areas were overrun with moonlighters illegally dumping toxic waste."

"It also paints Myron Sellers as some kind of local hero. You know, his moment of glory for fifteen minutes."

Jake shot the officer a curious look.

"I found a copy of the same article last night," said Slocum. "It was in an envelope along with articles from three or four local papers. At first, folks thought that truckers from New Jersey were hauling toxic waste up here. Turned out to be local haulers all the way."

"Big time?"

Slocum shook his head. "That's just the point. Small time, just like Winslow. My guess is the only reason it made the papers at all is because of him." He tapped the grainy image of Oliver Preston. "He was the news, not the few loads of chemicals that got dumped up in the mountains."

Jake scanned the rest of the article. "Sellers made arrests," he said.

"Even that didn't get anywhere." Slocum frowned. "I'm telling you, it was a botched deal right from the get-go. Sure, Myron brought some local guys in and tried to throw the book at them, but they all waltzed out the door."

"Not all of them" Jake said, putting down the newspaper, "The article mentions Russell Oaks went to trial."

Slocum nodded. "He got the worst of it. A fine and probation. Something like that."

"He still live around here?"

"Last I heard," Slocum answered and saw where the question led. "You don't think Russell had anything to do with this, do you?"

"Won't know until I talk to him," Jake said and asked for directions.

Watson painted the window with his nose, then sat in the front seat as Jake shifted into first, sending gravel chattering like rattlesnake tails in the fenders. Five miles past the village on a narrow, tree-lined lane, they turned onto Lyle Road, the unofficial end of Winslow proper.

The big white houses of the village center gave way to small, one-story rectangles. Some were trailers, added onto here and there at odd angles; some were empty and abandoned. Where someone still lived, snowmobiles and dismantled motorcycles lay uncovered in the front yard next to half-used woodpiles and sun-bleached plastic toys. Near the road, back from the shoulder, were country mailboxes—some leaning in, some leaning out, all victims of an errant snowplow blade. The one marked "Russell Oaks" was off the post, resting at the base of a tree.

Jake pulled into the dirt driveway and parked. A quick glance revealed a flat-roofed single-story house in need of repair and paint and a German shepherd chained to a makeshift doghouse. There were no cars, no trucks, and apparently no one at home.

"You stay," Jake told Watson and got out of the car. He kept his distance well outside the circle worn by the chained shepherd. He could feel the dog's eyes locking on him as he stepped toward the front door and knocked, and knocked again when no one answered.

"Anybody here?" he called out and knew instinctively that someone was. "My name's Jake Eaton. I'm a private investigator. I'd like to talk to Russell Oaks."

Silence.

Jake peered through the window at faint shadows as something moved inside. He knocked again, waited, then stepped off the porch to look around back just as the bony dog, back hair standing on end, hit the end of the chain, snarling and snapping. Stupid mutt, Jake thought as a hand parted the window curtains.

"There's no harm in talking," Jake hollered over the growls. "Besides, I can wait. I'm used to it. It's part of the job."

Slowly, cautiously, a silvery blonde opened the door. She was about thirty-five with light greenish gray eyes and a slight but very attractive figure. Her face was thin, and fair complected, and she had a full-lipped, even mouth. She was wearing faded jeans and a loose-fitting flannel shirt open at the neck.

"What do you want?" Her voice was as soft as the rest of her.

"A conversation," Jake said, surprised that such a beautiful creature could be found in such a hovel. This must be what it feels like to rub the bottle and find a genie, he thought. "Does Russell Oaks live here?"

"And if he does?"

"I'd like to speak with him."

"About what?" she asked coolly.

"That's between him and me."

"Not in this house. My husband and I have no secrets."

"And you are . . . ?"

"Elizabeth Oaks."

"Pleased," Jake said, tipping an imaginary hat as he stepped toward her. The woman's frozen expression didn't change. "Is he here?" Jake asked.

"This is about Myron Sellers, isn't it?"

"What makes you ask that?"

"What else would it be about?"

"The disappearance of Colin Owens." A curious look spread across her face. "Ever heard of him?" asked Jake.

"No."

"He worked for Milly Preston, Oliver's wife."

"I know who Mildreth Preston is," she said bitterly and tried to slam the door shut. Jake's foot kept it open. "My husband's not here," she snapped.

"I just want to ask him a few questions," Jake told her.

"And I suppose the police will, too."

"Maybe."

"Why don't you just leave us alone? All of you. Leave us be," she said, clutching the door with hands slender as tree roots and slamming it against Jake's foot. "We've done nothing wrong."

"I didn't say you had."

"Go back to wherever you came from," she said, pleading. "You know nothing about what goes on in Winslow. There's nothing for you to find, not even the truth."

"Then tell me the truth."

"It wouldn't do any good," she said and stepped back inside the house.

—9—

When Jake pulled up to the Inn at River Bend, a huge thunderhead was building over Winslow. A wind had come up and, although there was no thunder, lightning flickered inside the clouds like defective lightbulbs. Jake opened the door for the nervous Watson and followed him inside.

Lottie Ruggles was wiping clean the tables of the now empty bar. Without looking up, she informed Jake that Mrs. Preston was at the inn.

"She's waitin' in your room. With her money she won't steal nothin'," Lottie said with spite.

Jake didn't tolerate bitchy small-mindedness. "Mrs. Preston likes tea," he stated firmly.

Lottie stood straight up, glaring at him. "So?"

"So, bring her some." He wondered what miseries life had thrown her to make her so disagreeable. Jake and Watson climbed the stairs to the second floor.

Jake knocked and entered. Mildreth Gibbon Preston sat upright in the wing chair and looked perfectly comfortable with her half glasses resting low on her long, slender nose, her thin face framed by her neatly trimmed iron gray hair. She closed the book she'd been reading and set it aside as Watson trotted over and began nuzzling her hands.

"So we finally meet," she said and patted the friendly dog. "Your master didn't see fit to bring you along when I first met him, and now I know why. You're a show stealer."

Jake sat on the edge of the bed. "Watson's not fond of Beacon Hill. It's too finicky for his nature."

"I think Watson could get along anywhere, Mr. Eaton. I think you're the one who finds the Hill fussy and the people on it a temperamental match. Or do I hear something else in your voice?"

"Such as?"

She looked at him evenly. "I don't know. Perhaps you don't like my showing up unannounced."

Right on the button, Jake thought to himself and half smiled.

"Well, you'll get over it," she said confidently. "Besides, I couldn't very well stay home, could I? Not after that terrible business with Myron Sellers. What have you found out?"

"Not much."

"Exactly what Lieutenant Moreau said."

"You've been in touch?"

"I have. He seemed to pay a little more attention this time. Do I have you to thank for that?"

"We had a talk," Jake answered.

"As I expected. I liked that about you the moment we met. Here's a man who takes charge, who picks up the rock even though there might be a snake under it. It's a quality written all over your face even if it is banged about. What happened, may I ask?"

Jake told her about the attempted hit-and-run as a roll of thunder rattled the windows and sent Watson scurrying under the bed. "He looks like a dog, but he's a chicken at heart," Jake said, his affection for Watson showing through the tease.

"So I see." Mildreth seemed disappointed.

Watson looked embarrassed. His cowardice about thunderstorms was the dog's only weakness and one that Jake easily put up with. Outside, the wind picked up, and huge raindrops pelted the windows.

Jake pulled one knee up and clasped his hands around it. Rocking slightly forward, he asked Mrs. Preston how well she knew Myron Sellers.

"In what way?" she asked.

"I'm not sure. Back at your house you said you never quite trusted his motives. What did you mean by that?"

Mrs. Preston lifted a hankie to her lips and cleared her throat. "I meant," she said, "that Myron always seemed to behave as if he were trying to get even."

"With whom?"

"With anyone. I never felt he lifted a finger to help because he genuinely wanted to."

"Did he help you and Oliver?"

She nodded. "On occasion."

"How?"

She hesitated, not wanting to relive it. Shortly, she explained. "If you haven't already noticed, Winslow is an isolated village. Forty years ago, two people from Boston coming up here wasn't a signal for the locals to roll out the welcome mat. They ignored us at first, but once they sensed we weren't going away, things began happening."

"Like what?" Jake asked.

Mildreth seemed distracted. "Do you know what New Hampshire's state slogan is?" she asked.

"Live Free or Die."

"Correct. Live free. So simple when you say it, so difficult when you try it, because someone's always there tallying the expenses. But some things should not cost. Some things should be there for the taking." She paused. "On our property there's an underground stream with the purest water. Those who know about it won't drink anything else. I know we didn't. We'd take gallons back with us to Boston."

"I assume the villagers knew about it?" Jake asked.

As if she wished they hadn't, Mildreth replied, "They did."

"You don't sound too happy about it."

"I'm not. Years back," she said without sentiment, "someone threatened to poison it."

"Poison it?" The surprise showed in Jake's voice.

"Poison it," Mildreth repeated. "In our frequent and lengthy absences from Winslow, we hired Myron to watch over it for us. When Oliver died, I employed Myron to do so once more."

"Why?" Jake asked. "Were you threatened again?"

"Not in words, no. But I had a feeling. I can't explain it really, but when Oliver died, I wanted no one touching the land he so loved. I wanted no trespassers. Period."

"So Sellers kept everyone away."

"As far as I know, he did. Yes."

"What happened way back, when you first started coming to Winslow?"

"We'd park our car and go for a hike. When we'd get back, we'd likely as not find all our tires slashed. As we'd walk the two or so miles back into the village, people would greet us along the way with calls of 'Doctor Livingstone, I presume?' That sort of thing."

"What'd Sheriff Sellers do about any of this?"

"Nothing at first. We didn't ask for any help right off. We thought the pranks would die down, then go away. At least that's what we'd hoped."

"But they didn't."

"No. They got worse. We began to find tortured animals," she said and seemed to shrink back from the memory. "Birds with the top half of their beaks cut off, then tied to a branch to starve. Cats nailed to trees, dogs with their throats cut."

Jake glanced at Watson.

Mrs. Preston continued. "All done to shock us, to scare us away. But we didn't scare. Instead, we buried the animals and kept to ourselves. Finally, someone sent us a note saying if we didn't stay where we belonged, leave Winslow and go back to Boston, they'd poison the water. That's when we called in Myron."

"And," Jake said, "he put a quick stop to it."

Mildreth looked quizzically at Jake. "What makes you say that with such assurance?"

"Something the innkeeper said," Jake told her. "He said Sellers knew everything that went on in the village. It wouldn't take long to figure out who was causing you trouble."

"And it didn't."

"Was there an arrest?"

"No. There was never any arrest. The incidents simply stopped as quickly as they'd begun."

"But you must've had suspicions about who was behind it."

"We did, yes. Or I should say, Oliver did." Mrs. Preston let her eyes drift toward Watson, who still cowered under the bed. "I hesitate only because I saw the troublemaker's wife when I came in," Mrs. Preston said.

"Lottie Ruggles?" Jake asked, mildly astonished. "I wondered why she wasn't pleased to see you."

Mildreth nodded. "I felt that myself. But even Lottie must've known that her husband, John, was capable of anything. Especially if it made somebody else's life less pleasant."

There was a brisk knock on the door. Jake stood and opened it.

"You wanted tea?" Kenney Ruggles made it sound like a bilious request with his heavy, sullen voice.

"Put it on the table," Jake told him.

Kenney did, with a look that taunted Mildreth Preston with each step. "Anything else?" he asked her.

Mildreth stared right back at him. "Do you have something to say to me, young man?"

Kenney shifted his weight from one foot to the other. "My mother sends her regards," he said and left, closing the door behind him.

In the uneasy silence that followed, Jake poured a cup of tea and handed it to Mildreth.

"He looks just like his father," she said. "And that cold and unforgiving voice. It's uncanny."

"He forgot the cream," Jake said.

"I doubt it." Her voice was harsh. "More likely he just didn't bring it," she said, then pursed her lips. "I'm sorry. I don't mean to be so petty. What is it the psychiatrists say? If you can't deal with it, avoid it. I've tried to put that in practice when it comes to the Ruggles family. I haven't thought of them in years."

"Because of Old John?"

"That, and I suppose I had my feelings hurt." She sipped her tea and set down the cup. "Thank you for the tea."

"My pleasure."

"Do you know how Old John died?"

"Suicide."

"Yes. It was terrible, really, and I was concerned about his children and what emotional tempests might be building up in them.

Contrary to what some may think, I am not a busybody. I simply wanted Mrs. Ruggles to know that Oliver and I had friends at Harvard who were professionals in the field of how youngsters deal with the death of a parent. I offered to make the names available if she wanted them."

"And she didn't?"

"No," Mrs. Preston said stiffly.

"Because she thought you were a busybody," Jake suggested.

"It would seem so. She didn't say. I went to her home to explain my concern, and she slammed the door in my face. That was the end of it. Except," she added thoughtfully, "it wasn't really. Something like that never leaves you, does it? It lingers in the back of the mind, like some dark shadow."

"Care to shine some light on it?"

"In what regard?"

"John and Lottie Ruggles's kids. What drew you to them?"

"Children in need are children in need, Mr. Eaton. Even if I'd wanted to, I couldn't turn my back on them. They weren't the cause of our village troubles, and I wasn't going to make them suffer as if they were."

Admirable, Jake thought. The world would be a hell of a lot better off with more people in it like Mildreth Gibbon Preston. For good or bad, Jake would never be one of them, and he knew it. Making people suffer was part of his job.

"How many kids were there?" he asked finally.

"Two. Kenney and his sister. She was the one who found her father's body. Imagine what a nineteen year old must have felt walking into her own house on the night of her senior prom and finding her father lying there dead. It's unforgivable. Choosing that night of all nights to kill himself seemed particularly cruel."

Not if he was the bastard everyone made him out to be, Jake thought. "What happened to the girl?" he asked.

"The same thing that happens to most who stay their lives in villages such as this. She got married right out of high school and started a family."

"There are worse ways to spend your life," Jake commented.

"Oh, don't get me wrong," Mrs. Preston backtracked. "I'm in

favor of marriage. I wish I still were married, but that's not the point."

A bolt of lightning flashed across the darkened sky. "What is the point?" Jake asked.

She shifted in her seat and straightened her back as if about to begin a lecture. "The point is not just to marry, but to marry well. In a village this small, the odds are against that happening. The Ruggles girl is a case in point. She was so beautiful, and with the proper education, she could have had the pick of the lot. Instead, she married Russell Oaks."

The name sped through Jake's mind like fire. "Russell Oaks?"

Mildreth nodded. "Do you know him?"

"Haven't had the pleasure. I did meet his wife. She's one very frightened lady."

"My heart went out to that young woman," Mildreth added.

"You sound disappointed."

"A waste of young life is always disappointing."

"Did Oliver feel the same way?"

Mildreth's chin jutted out defensively. "Why do you ask?"

Jake shrugged. "I don't know. You said yourself that Oliver was in love with the world. I just thought he might be more forgiving of those who lived in it."

"Russell Oaks, for example?" Mildreth asked bitterly.

"You tell me."

"I can't." She looked at Jake, the past hurt shining through her eyes. "It was one of the few times in our marriage when Oliver wouldn't confide in me."

"What was he holding back?"

"I never knew. He died without ever saying, but there was something about what happened up in these mountains that Oliver never quite got over. It changed him, Jake. But it changed him in a way I didn't like."

Mildreth's words sent a prickle of uneasiness along Jake's spine. "Something more than the dump sites?" he asked.

"I don't know. The sites themselves were a crushing blow. Oliver thought of the mountains as a private Eden. Then Russell and his ilk came along and spoiled it. I have pictures of it all, you know," she said offhandedly. "For the Oaks trial, Oliver had aerial photographs taken of the contaminated areas just before we cleaned them all up."

"Photographs?" The word seemed somehow magnetic, as if pulling together pieces of the puzzle. "Of your property?"

"The parts that were contaminated, yes. But most of the sites were on others' land, not ours."

"What do these pictures show?"

"Poisoned land the size of football fields where the chemicals were poured out onto the ground. They look like dry, dark lake beds. Barren, every one of them," she said sadly.

"I'd like to see them," Jake told her.

"Of course."

"What about the photographs that Colin Owens took? Did you get prints of those before he disappeared?" Jake asked.

"I did," Mildreth answered. "They're all at home. You may look through them, but not until after Myron's funeral tomorrow afternoon. I'll be going back then. You're free to come along."

Jake knew there was no point in trying to get her to go now, so he didn't argue. He stepped to the window. The storm outside was intensifying. "Do you know who took the aerials for the Oaks trial?" Jake asked.

"I don't. Oliver handled all that. But I do think he sought advice from Gloria's father. She and F. Gordon spent quite a bit of time up here then. Oliver would have asked his advice."

"Why would F. Gordon have any insight?" Jake wondered aloud. "GC has a corporate jet, but that's about it as far as pilots go."

"True now, but back then F. Gordon was acquiring land holdings all around the country."

"And he hired aerial surveyors," Jake said knowingly as a crack of thunder sent Watson further under the bed. "My partner obviosly doesn't like storms," Jake said, picking up his jacket. "Mind looking after him for a while?"

"Not at all, but where are you going in this weather?"

"To the airport."

Mildreth looked out the window at the rain sheeting down the glass. "Those little planes won't be flying in this."

"That's what I'm counting on," Jake said, bending down to Watson. "Keep an eye on our client," he said to the nervous dog. Jake gave him a pat. "You're in charge," he told him and left.

The airport was closed as expected, the small planes grounded because of the violent spring storm. Jake parked in front of the Quonset hut where Jason Malone had his office and dodged puddles on his run to the door. Inside, a middle-aged woman looking every bit the picture of authority glanced up from her computer screen.

"May I help you?" she asked.

"I'd like to see Mr. Malone."

"He's busy."

"He's playing cards. Hardest work you can get."

"And your name?"

"Jake Eaton."

She picked up the phone and buzzed the inner office. "As you expected, Mr. Malone, he's here. Yes, the private detective." She hung up and went back to her keyboard. In seconds, Jason Malone stepped out from his private office and closed the door behind him.

"I knew you'd show up," Malone said. "Something told me when the rains came, you'd be close behind. Especially with the game changing from missing person to murder." He removed his cap and ran his fingers through his oily hair. "Damn," he said, shaking his head. "That changes things, you know?"

"Murder always does," Jake told him.

"A list of names to talk to about somebody missing is one thing. But murder? That's pretty heavy, Eaton. Fact is I don't have the names for you." He put his cap back on and moved toward the window. "I'm not getting them either."

Jake followed him. "I'm only after *one* name."

"And that is?"

"You said before that early on in Colin's career, he got in money trouble so deep the bank took back his plane."

"That's right. It drove him out of business."

"You also said it worked out for the best, that in no time Colin was back in the money."

"That's right. He was."

"Who'd he go to work for?" Jake asked.

Surprise crept through Malone's expression. "Is that the name you want?"

"It is for the time being."

"But that was fifteen or twenty years ago," Malone protested. "I can't remember that far back."

"Try."

"I don't know . . ."

Jake took a fifty-dollar bill from his wallet. He handed it to Jason Malone. "Add this to the pot. It might help your memory."

Malone put the bill in his pocket. "Memory about what?"

"Who flew the survey for Oliver Preston."

"Oliver?" Malone's expression clouded in doubt.

"Never heard of him?"

"Sure I've heard of him. The man's dead. That's what this memorial is all about."

"Could be what Colin's disappearance and Sellers's murder are all about, too. See what you can find out. I'll be in touch," Jake told him and headed out the door.

—10—

The rain slowed on the drive back to the inn and Jake put the wipers on intermittent. His mind seemed to work in similar start and stop motions, jumping between the disappearance of Colin Owens, the death of Myron Sellers, and thoughts of Gloria Gorham. For some reason, he couldn't get her out of his mind tonight. Maybe because in some small way, she was part of Winslow.

He imagined her walking the mountains surrounding the village, jumping rock to rock over the clear, running streams. He saw her as a happy child, laughing and spinning wildly around with arms stretched toward the bright blue sky as if holding it up with all her promise. Then, with one sweep of the wipers, he saw her as she was, damaged and struggling to emerge whole once again.

What was Gloria doing now? he wondered. What wooden boat project had she concocted to fill her hours, to help her forget? You're going to have to join the real world sometime, he'd told her. You can't hide on *Gamecock* forever. But the truth was, with her wealth, she could do whatever she wanted, including digging a luxurious hole and crawling in. Giving up was one thing about her he couldn't comprehend. For him, quitting was never an option.

Jake slowed for the inn, pulled in, and parked. He shut off the Saab's engine and got out. The rain had stopped, and the heavy clouds were breaking apart near the mountaintops.

He climbed the steps and went inside to the lobby to call

Gloria. He wanted privacy, not Mrs. Preston looking over his shoulder as he talked. The phone rang eight times before Gloria picked up with a soft hello. Jake released a breath at the sound of her welcome voice. "Me again," he said.

"Jake!"

"One and the same."

"Are you back in Cambridge?"

"I wish."

"Soon?"

"Maybe sooner if I can get you to do me a favor." He waited, afraid the ploy was too transparent.

"What sort of favor?" Gloria finally asked.

"Ask a few questions for me." He could feel her hesitancy through the phone. "Nothing too unpleasant," he said encouragingly. "Milly Preston—"

"Mildreth Gibbon Preston."

Jake smiled. "I stand corrected."

"How are you two getting along?" Gloria asked, deftly changing the subject.

"Fine. She's up here in my room as we speak. She said your father suggested a surveyor to Oliver."

"I wouldn't know anything about that."

"I didn't think you would. But I was wondering if you'd check into it for me. See if you could find out who it was."

"Me?"

Jake could sense that she was about to reject the notion. "You could take your father out for drinks," he offered. "Nothing special, just an evening out."

"I don't think I should, Jake."

Jake wouldn't let her say no. "It'll only take a few minutes. Dress up a little bit and take him out. Do you both good."

Her reply was short and quick. "No."

"You know he's worried about you." Jake paused, then said, "You know we're all thinking about you." He couldn't bring himself to say more. "I'll call tomorrow and see how it's going."

"I'm not doing it, Jake."

"Say around five."

"I'm not."

"And say hello to F. Gordon for me."

"You're not listening. I'm not going to help you." She paused, thinking. "Jake?"

"Yeah?"

"I appreciate what you're trying to do. I really do. I just can't help you. Bye, Jake," she said and put down the phone.

Jake hung up. He expected to feel triumphant and clever at his attempt to get Gloria to rejoin life. Instead he felt deflated, his proposition defeated by a woman not yet ready to act.

Jake stepped to the bar where Danny Dodge was brewing a fresh pot of coffee. Dodge offered a cup, but Jake declined.

"You look like you could use something," Dodge commented. "Any progress?"

Jake's thoughts were still on his conversation with Gloria. "Too soon to tell." He ordered a vodka gimlet on the rocks and watched Dodge go to work.

Dodge dropped a lime slice in the glass and set the drink in front of Jake. "You staying around for the funeral?" Dodge wanted to know.

"I am."

"I hate funerals."

"They're not my favorite pastime," Jake said, sipping his cocktail.

"What is? When you're not catching bad guys, what do you do?" Dodge asked.

"Practice being an optimist."

Dodge frowned. "I'm serious," he said.

"So am I," Jake answered. "My brother used to say life is great if you don't give up."

"I'd say he's right." Dodge wiped his hands dry and put the towel in front of him on the bar. "I've always felt my wife would be running this place with me if she hadn't done just that."

"Just what?"

"Given up. Her doctor said she wanted to die, so she let go. I stepped out of the hospital room for a coffee, came back ten minutes later, and she was dead. She'd run out of fight, I guess."

"Some people don't have much to begin with," Jake said. "Some who do can lose it. There aren't any easy answers."

"I guess your brother would agree with that, too. Is he a private cop?"

"Was." Jake took another drink. "He was murdered on the job."

"Sorry."

"So am I." Jake finished his gimlet and stood. "There'll be two of us for dinner."

Dodge grinned, pleased the topic had changed. "Mrs. Preston has already made the reservation," he said. "It's at eight."

"At eight?"

"Yes. She's a very determined woman. She even selected the table in the corner by the window. Wouldn't sit anywhere else."

"Best to please her," Jake conceded.

"I'm not sure that's possible," Dodge said. "There're some women men can never please, and Milly Preston looks like one of them to me."

"You an expert on women, are you, Mr. Dodge?" Jake asked skeptically.

"Not at all. And you?"

"I'm an amateur, just like the rest of us," Jake said and went up to his room.

—11—

Eric Bramble, the bald, heavyset Methodist minister, grabbed the lectern with one fat hand, pushed his bifocals back up his spreading red nose with the other, looked kindly over the full church, and continued.

"We know not why God lifted this good man to heaven. We know only that it was done, that Myron was raised up into the Kingdom to sit beside our Lord. All of us—family, friends, neighbors in need as we all were—are saddened by our loss but gladdened at the thought that our sheriff now lives in eternal and restful peace. Have mercy on his spirit, Lord. Forgive him his sins. Let us pray. Our Father, who . . ."

The congregation rose, its singular voice falling in behind the minister's. Jake stood in the back, silently eyeing the crowd.

As funerals go, this wasn't bad. Winslow showed its respect by closing down and filling the church. Jake imagined that Sellers would have been pleased with the turnout even though one of those who strolled by the open casket probably killed him. Jake wondered what the killer thought looking down at the makeup that was once the man. Sorrow? Joy? Remorse? Panic? Maybe relief that so far he'd gotten away with firing a rifle that sent a bullet through the skin causing so much confusion that life ran out of Myron Sellers.

The prayer ended. The crowd sat back down and waited, motionless. Even the children who'd been dressed up and dragged away from their play did not move. Reverend Bramble cleared his throat.

"Our little village sheriff had much good in him, Lord. Many of us will attest to that. An act of kindness, a touch of caring— Myron Sellers was always there to help." Bramble paused and looked out across the flock.

"But who was there to help him on that tragic afternoon?" he asked solemnly. "Our limited mortal vision can see no explanation for his tragic death, Lord. Our limited mortal vision sees only Myron Sellers full of life, defending his community from the forces of evil, helping his fellow man walk the right path, only to die alone in the line of duty in the office he'd held for many, many years. Yet, there is a reason for this, Lord. All of us know that this emptiness in our hearts has purpose. The family's suffering has meaning. Comfort is coming, we know. Comfort is coming and we await it with open hearts. We trust Your vision, Lord. We trust Your vision and will try to understand Your wisdom in taking Myron into Your arms. Let us sing."

The voices rose, some cracking through tears, others booming toward the heavens. When the music stopped, the double doors opened and the people filed out into the bright afternoon sun.

Mildreth Gibbon Preston—stately in her tailored black suit— comforted Cora Sellers, Myron's wife, as the coffin was loaded into the hearse for the short drive to the cemetery. Many walked, including Lottie Ruggles. Even dressed up, she was not a pretty woman: thin from the neck up and the knees down and pear shaped in the middle.

Lottie knew there was little hope of making herself attractive. Long ago she gave up dabbing color on her cheeks; she went out looking chalky and pale, as if a ghost had crossed her path. In her mind there was a ghost: her long-dead husband. Able Singer said that Old John—something Lottie never called him—haunted the Ruggles's house, but it was Lottie he haunted. Not that she was sorry he was dead.

Over their twenty-plus years of marriage, her feelings for John had dried up like a sun-baked seashell. Even her tears were gone.

Nothing was left but a slight pang of regret over the mess he'd made taking his leave. A mess of puddled blood she'd cleaned as best she could and thought of each time she swept a guest room at the inn. The fact was she hated Old John for what he'd done and for what he left her with: two kids and a future spent on her knees at the Inn at River Bend. The thought made her blood boil.

But there were glimmers of hope. After the shock of her father's suicide had worn away, Elizabeth blossomed into a beautiful young woman. She'd married Russell Oaks, her childhood sweetheart, and had two healthy children. Russell would never win any prizes for quick wit, but he was steady, and from what Lottie could tell, still in love with Elizabeth and the two girls.

Then there was Kenney. No matter how much Lottie bitched and hollered at him to make something of himself, he simply set his jaw and stared back at her as if her influence as a mother evaporated once he became a man.

At first she blamed Kenney's lack of interest in life on Old John's suicide. If the father loved life so little, what could be expected of the son? Not much, she thought while trying daily to set some fire under him. Kenney—gloomy and angry at the world—always put it out.

Kenney was the downturn that broke his mother's heart—the constant reminder of where life had brought her, with no way out. Maybe Myron Sellers—quietly smiling in his box—has it better than some of the living, she thought as she made her way to the cemetery.

"Mind if I walk along?" Jake asked as he caught up to Lottie.

"And if I do?"

Jake let her iciness pass. "I wanted to thank you for letting Mrs. Preston in my room."

"Just doing my job," she said not breaking her stride. "Wouldn't want the lady to think we didn't know our place now, would we?"

"And what place is that?" Jake asked.

Lottie eyed Jake bitterly. "Don't play games. You know how white trash is treated."

"From what I was told, Mrs. Preston only tried to help."

"She tell you we go back a ways, did she?"

"She did."

"People in Winslow take care of their own. If she was so smart, she'd know that. All you got to do is look around."

"No one helped Sheriff Sellers," Jake reminded her.

"So?"

"So maybe Winslow's not so helpful after all."

"I never ask for help from outsiders. Simple as that," Lottie said and put an end to the discussion.

They walked in silence until Jake commented, "Shame about Sellers."

"Some would say."

"Not you?" Jake asked.

Lottie stopped abruptly. "I just do rooms. That's what's asked of me, that's what I do. If there's a problem with the way I do yours, talk to the innkeeper. He's a fair man, which is more than I'll say for most. Now, I'm here to see Sellers off."

"And I'm trying to find out who killed him."

"I can't help you."

"You could answer a few questions."

"I could. I don't care to."

"If he was a friend of yours—"

"I didn't say that. I said I was here to see him put in the ground and forgotten. He wasn't a saint; he was a man with faults like all the rest."

"A sheriff with faults collects enemies," Jake said.

"I suppose. I know I hated him; I suppose others did, too," Lottie said and continued walking.

"Why?"

"None of your business."

"Did you hate him enough to kill him?"

"Most likely. But I didn't."

"You just *happened* to see me go in his office about the time he was shot, that it?"

Lottie glared at him. "I was taking my afternoon walk, Mr. Eaton. I've taken it for years. Every day. Up the same road, past Sellers's office to the last house on the left, then back to the inn. Ask Mr. Dodge, if you or that lieutenant haven't already. When I

went by Myron's office, I saw you go in, and I said so once I heard
he'd been shot."

Jake increased his pace to keep up with her quickening gait.
"Any chance you also saw someone else and failed to mention it?"
he asked.

"No."

"Look," Jake said. "I read an article about Russell's troubles. I
know about his run-in with the sheriff."

Lottie's eyes narrowed to slits. "So?"

Jake shrugged off her glare. "So it seems a little odd that right
after the man who busted him gets shot, Russell's nowhere to be
found."

Lottie stopped abruptly. "I didn't see Russell Oaks anywhere
near that office, if that's what you're asking," she snapped. "I saw
you. But that doesn't matter, does it? You folks from the big city
have it your way no matter what the facts are."

"What are you talking about?" Jake asked genuinely.

"Oliver Preston. As if you didn't know."

"What about him?"

"He twisted Sellers around his little finger. Big shot from Harvard comes up here and buys a mountain. Can you believe that?"
She shook her head in amazement. "Most folks in the village
thought he was crazy. There're mountains all over the damn
place—who needs to own one? Oliver and his wife may have been
a big deal down your way, but up here they were just two fools sep-
arated from their money."

"Is money what drew Sellers to the Prestons?"

"You seem to know our village sheriff real well," she said scorn-
fully. "Money always got Myron's attention."

"Yet he and the Prestons became good friends."

"Myron Sellers had no friends."

"The church was full," Jake reminded her. "Somebody cared."

"Like Mildreth Preston?" Her voice was sharp, bitter. She
pointed her finger at Jake. "Let me tell you something. The Prestons used Sellers for all they could, and he did the same back
to them. Each using the other like it was the most natural thing
in the world. Russell Oaks got caught in the middle, and that's
a fact."

"How'd he get caught in the middle?" Jake asked.

"I've said too much already," Lottie told him and continued walking.

"Maybe Russell decided it was time to get even," Jake said, matching her steps.

"I knew that was the answer you were looking for," she said with a sneer. "Blame it on Russell. He's an easy target. All you want folks to do is forget you were there. Forget you could've done it."

Jake ignored her. "I'm looking for the truth," he said as Lottie again stopped cold in her tracks.

"There is no truth in Winslow. Myron Sellers saw to that," she said bitterly and stormed off toward Elizabeth and her two children waiting near the sheriff's grave.

A knot formed in Jake's stomach as he watched her go. What had boiled into bitterness in that woman? he wondered as Lieutenant Moreau broke away from the ambling crowd and joined him.

"Nice service," Moreau said. "Too bad there had to be one, especially a police officer and all, but a nice service just the same." He was talking to himself and knew it. "What are you thinking about?" he asked eventually.

"Lottie Ruggles," Jake said, looking at Moreau. "She just said the same thing her daughter told me hours ago."

"And what's that?"

"There's no truth in Winslow. What do you suppose that means, Lieutenant?"

"I have no idea," Moreau admitted, looking around. "Where's your pooch?" he asked.

"On duty," Jake told him.

"Really?"

"Really," Jake said. "How much do you know about Lottie's husband?"

"Quite a bit. That is, if you're asking about his suicide."

"I am."

Moreau reached into his coat pocket and took out a small notebook. "I pulled the file on one John Stanley Ruggles yesterday right after I spoke to Lottie. She didn't want to talk about it."

"Do you blame her?"

"Probably not. It was pretty messy all around," the lieutenant said and looked at his notes. "It was senior prom night, sixteen years ago. Lottie and Kenney—then four—were in the church basement that night. Lottie was on the prom refreshment committee. She took Kenney with her. Old John stayed home to keep the TV company and to drink himself to sleep. At midnight, the dance ended and the cleanup committee took over. The trash was to be dumped into Old John's pickup, but John didn't show. Elizabeth and her date—Russell Oaks—went to the house to see why and found him dead in the living room with one shot in his head. Myron Sellers was the first official on the scene. He called the medical examiner, who pronounced him dead by his own hand."

"Was there an autopsy?"

"There was. Blood analysis showed he was legally drunk and then some."

"Did he leave a note?" Jake asked.

Moreau looked in his notebook and quoted, "'Forgive me, Lottie. I don't know what else to do.'"

"Forgiveness for what?"

Moreau shrugged. "I don't know. For being a drunk, I'd guess. From what I gather, he was a bastard to be around. You can imagine how he was to live with." Moreau closed the notebook and slipped it back in his pocket. "Officer Slocum said you went to see Russell Oaks."

"That's right."

"How'd you make out?"

"Couldn't find him," Jake said.

"Neither could I."

Jake kicked at a tuft of grass with his toe. "You following me around, Lieutenant?"

"Just doing police work. Oaks was on my list of suspects."

"Who else is?" Jake wanted to know.

"A local no-good by the name of Joey Barns and"—Moreau hesitated, then said—"Colin Owens."

"Owens?"

Moreau nodded. "It's a possibility."

"It's a reach. A prayer."

"Maybe, but it answers one big question."

Jake kicked at the grass again. "I know the question, Lieutenant, and I know the answer."

"Fire away."

"Where'd Myron Sellers come up with two thousand bucks? Answer—Colin Owens."

Moreau nodded, smiling. "When you told me about the airport card games, I did a little checking. Every time Colin sat at the table, Sellers was one of the players. The way I figure it, Colin got tired of losing so much to Sellers and decided to put an end to it."

"Gamblers are rarely killers, Lieutenant. Besides, when Owens disappeared every cop in two states was out looking for him. A man bent on murder wouldn't draw that kind of attention to himself. Owens might have his hand in this, but not as the killer."

"A hand in how?" Moreau questioned.

"In the only two ways we know about: card games and photographs."

"So?"

"So, I'm driving back to Boston to look at those photographs . . ." Jake's explanation died on his lips as a green Mercedes crested the small hill and eased to a stop a few feet away.

Jake stepped around Moreau and walked to the car. Moreau followed, cringing as Mildreth Gibbon Preston rolled down the driver's window.

"I think you two know each other," Jake said, as if introducing two fighting cats.

Moreau pulled in a deep breath and let it out slowly. "Mrs. Preston," he mumbled with a nod and walked away.

Mildreth managed a curt smile, then shifted her attention to Jake. "Are you sure this is what you want?" she asked, stroking Watson's neck. Watson was sitting beside her in the front seat clearly enjoying the creature comforts of the Mercedes, and the added attention. "I don't mind driving back alone. I'm perfectly capable."

"I never had any doubt," Jake told her. "Are you ready?"

"I am."

Jake spotted a tan Ford pulling to a stop beside the church

some fifty yards away. "Just remember what we agreed on," he cautioned Mildreth as he kept his eyes on the tan car.

"Of course," she said and drove off.

When she had gone, Jake caught up to Moreau. He motioned toward the Ford. "Ever seen that car around here, Lieutenant?"

"Not that I recall."

They walked toward the car. The driver got out. "Our business is with Eaton," he said.

"It's all right, Lieutenant," Jake commented and approached the car. Moreau stopped, wary of the increased tension. Jake cut a quick glance at the man still in the front seat. He was looking for the man's hands and found them empty.

"That's close enough," the driver said. He looked to be about two hundred fifty pounds and about six foot four.

Jake stopped in front of the man. "I think you boys should slack off on the weight lifting and put in a few more hours making a good tail. I spotted you as soon as I left Terry Owens's house."

The man ignored the wisecrack. "We're here with an invitation."

"Neither one of you is my partying type."

"You're working for the wrong client."

"That so?"

"Frazer Woodbine thinks it is. Mr. Woodbine is usually right."

"Never heard of him," Jake remarked.

Jake saw the 9mm automatic strapped to the man's side when he lifted his arm to check the time. "It's two-thirty. Mr. Woodbine says for you to come by at four. Sharp." The man handed Jake an address and climbed back into his car. "And Eaton, sharp means sharp."

"Never any doubt in my mind," Jake said as the Ford fishtailed off.

Moreau walked up in the dust. "What the hell was that all about?" he asked.

Jake wrote down the license plate number. "Seems Frazer Woodbine would like to meet me."

"Woodbine?"

"You heard of him?"

"Not positive, but I think he owns property somewhere around here."

"Wouldn't hurt to check that," Jake said, handing the plate number to Moreau. "See what you can find out about this, too."

"You got it." Moreau put the paper in his pocket.

"Now I'm off to Boston," said. Jake. "I've got to get there before Milly Preston does."

—12—

As Jake had requested, Mildreth Gibbon Preston sought out back roads and stayed under the speed limits even though it bruised her ego; she didn't want to look like a lost old lady. She had never learned to take orders easily, never learned to slow down. As she negotiated the turns up the mountain named for her and Oliver, it seemed too late for her to learn now, but she was doing her best to follow instructions. Watson sat beside her mindful of his responsibility to keep Mildreth Preston safe. No one would get in her car, and she would not get out.

While Watson's mind was on business, Mrs. Preston's wandered. She had developed over the years a conviction that Winslow—not the village but the mountains surrounding it—were the most beautiful creations on earth. Where else in the world were there such stands of pine and hardwood? Such pure running water and robust rhododendrons? Where else on a winter's night could the north wind give the sky the acoustics of a seashell? And, in spring, the thunder rolling across the mountains seemed loud enough to rattle the angels in heaven.

It was indeed a magnificent place, she thought, and pulled over for a peaceful look around. She parked on an old logging road and turned off the ignition. As she reached for the door handle, Watson's spine hairs rose stiff as a boar's bristles. He let out a low rumble and gently swatted at her hand with his meaty paw.

Mrs. Preston looked stunned at the turn of events. "I beg your pardon?" she queried the dog, matching him in a glaring contest. "You're not going to let me out, are you?"

Watson nosed her hand away from the door.

"Well, all right," she said, thinking Jake may know best. She gave Watson one final look. "And I don't mean it's all right for you to treat me this way," she told the dog. "Because it's not."

Watson kept his eyes on her hands. When she moved one to the key and started the car, he sat back down, his eyes on the road as Mrs. Preston drove slowly along.

Jake drove south like a madman. He was always more comfortable acting on clear, logical thinking rather than hunches, but something told him that Mildreth shouldn't be alone in her house. He told her as much, but her plan was to go home after the service. Regardless of what Jake said, no matter the seriousness with which it was conveyed, she was going home. So Jake provided Watson as her bodyguard; meanwhile, he drove his Saab furiously toward Beacon Hill.

The overriding thought seemingly trapped in Jake's brain concerned aerial photographs. The chaos in Winslow began after Mildreth hired Colin Owens to take them. Those pictures and the ones Oliver had taken before were the only physical evidence linking Colin, Myron Sellers, and Russell Oaks to Preston Mountain. Jake had a hunch that he wasn't the only one who might find that fact a magnet to Milly's Boston home. The hunch had a name: Russell Oaks.

Jake didn't slow to the speed limit until he saw the traffic jam on Route 128 heading south outside of Boston. He snaked through as best he could, then hit five miles of open space on Route 2 before the rotaries near Fresh Pond slowed him to a frustrating crawl. Storrow Drive permitted some weaving room to Charles Street. From there, it was an easy five blocks to Brimmer Street, where he skidded to a stop next to the police cruiser that blocked the intersection.

"Hey!" The officer in blues barked like Watson. "You can't park there!"

"I'm private," Jake told him and held out his license.

"Who gives a damn?"

"I've got a case on this block."

"And we've got a robbery in progress. Move your car and get the hell outta here."

"Which house?" Jake pressed.

"You don't listen, do ya?" the cop said, stepping back to let an unmarked move through. Sergeant William Riley was in the passenger seat.

"What the hell you doing here, Jake?" Riley asked.

"Looking out for my client."

"Who is it?"

Jake identified her.

Riley opened the back door. "Get in," he said. Jake parked his car and jumped in with Riley. They drove fifty yards to the front of the yellow and white four-story mansion.

"Bet they're not stealing dollhouses," Jake said.

"Say again?"

Jake told Riley about the dollhouse that Milly Preston kept in the living room. Riley—fiftyish, round-faced, and fifteen pounds too heavy—scowled at the news. "I'm not interested in dollhouses," he stated flatly.

"No," Jake said. "I didn't figure you were."

Riley's extra fifteen pounds had been around for as long as Jake had known him. Riley's belly stretched the buttons on his blue button-down Oxford shirt. The top button was open, the striped tie sagged to the right, the brown Harris tweed jacket had patches covering the elbows.

Riley got out of the car. Jake followed. "Damn near didn't recognize you without Watson. Give him the day off, did you?" Riley teased.

"He's with Milly Preston." Jake pointed. "That's her house," he said.

"I know whose house it is." Riley looked over the building and drew his weapon. "It's just the kind of place these guys like to hit. We've had eight burglaries on the Hill in the past six months. Nothing but the best homes. Two men, in and out, slick as you please. They leave the reproductions and cart off the good stuff."

"Sounds like real pros."

"You got it. Last time they cut a forty thousand dollar crystal chandelier out of a ceiling." Riley couldn't hide his admiration. "They walked out in broad daylight like your normal everyday contractor." Riley turned to Jake. "But you couldn't know any of that," Riley said. "Yet, here you are. Why?"

"Mrs. Preston's out of town."

"That's what the neighbor said who called this in. Still, you haven't answered my question. What are you doing here, Jake? Business so bad you're guarding homes now?"

"Business is fine."

"You're still not answering the question."

"You heard about that part-time sheriff who was killed a few days ago in New Hampshire?"

"Yeah, I heard."

"Mildreth Preston is driving back from his funeral. It crossed my mind that somebody might pay her a visit while she was out of the house."

"You got names?"

"Only a hunch," Jake said as the crack of gunfire sounded from the alley.

Instantly, Riley dropped to a two-handed shooting position, his service revolver aimed at the house. "Epstein's around back," he said, focusing on movement inside.

Jake raced down the street, around the corner, and through the alley where Saul Epstein, a veteran officer of thirty years, stood shaking his head.

"Fucking kid." Epstein held his forearm; still, the blood trickled over his hand.

"You all right?" Jake asked.

Epstein nodded and rolled his palm up. He'd been hit just below the elbow in the muscle.

"He came out the back. I identified myself as a police officer, then he ducked behind the white car. Next thing I know, he fires one round and takes off down the alley. Nothing more than a punk kid. I should've known better, but the M.O. on these guys is strictly walking away with the jewels. No hard stuff. So, how do you figure?"

"Wrong guys," Jake said.

"My luck."

"Where'd he go?"

"Left at the end of the alley's all I saw. Could be in China by now." Epstein made sure everything still worked by opening and closing his fist. "It's gonna hurt like hell in the morning."

"Always does," Jake said and started slowly down the alley.

"Only one came out, Jake. The other one's still inside."

"I'll be careful."

Over the thick silence of the city, Jake heard Riley's amplified voice warning whoever was inside to come out, hands clasped behind his head. No one would get hurt. Jake waited, then moved on when he was sure there were no takers.

At the back of the Preston house was a service porch covered with latticework painted dark green. Jake broke into a sweat as he eased around a red BMW and sprinted to the porch door. It was ajar and opened wider when he reached up and nudged it with the barrel of his drawn .38.

A surge of adrenaline swept through him as he climbed the first step and reached cautiously for the second. The door to the kitchen was ten feet away across the wooden porch. He hurried to it and had his hand on the knob when the door flew open. A heavyset man burst through it, knocking Jake down the steps. Jake's gun slipped from his hand and clattered across the alley.

Jake was rubber legged and dazed. When he tried to get up, the man charged him like a bull and slammed him into the BMW. Jake's head snapped back against the car window and filled with a wildly surging pain. As he sagged to the pavement, he heard Epstein's voice calling for the man to halt.

Don't shoot, thought Jake. Let me talk to him. Let me . . .

The first shot went far to the left as Epstein overcompensated for his throbbing forearm, but the second killed Jake's attacker and he fell to the ground.

Jake was on his feet before the medics arrived. As a precaution, the ambulance attendants strapped Epstein on a stretcher, then checked Jake for a concussion. They left for the hospital with Epstein as patrol cars came and went. Police officers spread throughout the neighborhood, asking questions, and reporters waited and rehearsed in front of their cameras. The medical examiner spoke briefly to Sergeant Riley while the official pictures were taken of the crime scene. When the photographer finished, the medical examiner began his work on the body. Riley moved to Jake, who was sitting on a step feeling the lump on his skull.

"How's the head?" Riley asked.

"Hurts, but it's been worse."

Riley rocked from heel to toe. "Did you know the guy who ran you over?"

"Thought I did," Jake said flatly.

"Meaning?"

"Meaning Russell Oaks is in his thirties. This guy looked—"

"This guy," Riley broke in, "was over fifty, and his name wasn't Oaks. It was Owens. Colin Owens."

Jake rubbed the knot and winced. "Owens?"

"Then you do know him," Riley surmised. "What's this all about, Jake?"

"I wish the hell I knew. All I can tell you for sure is that Colin Owens disappeared about two weeks ago. I was hired to find him."

"By?"

"Mildreth Preston."

"So that's what you're doing here," Riley said and turned to an officer Jake didn't know. "Check the house top to bottom," Riley told him. "See if you can locate Mrs. Preston, then—"

"She's out front," Jake said.

"How do you know?"

"I didn't want her coming home alone, so I asked her to wait for me in her car a block down on Brimmer."

"From what I've heard," Riley said, "Mrs. Preston does what the hell she pleases."

Jake smiled knowingly. "Watson's with her."

"Keeping her in the car, is he?" Riley knew Watson as well as Jake. "You've got one hell of a partner, Eaton. If you ever want to give him up—"

"Not a chance."

Riley turned to a waiting officer. "Find Mrs. Preston. Have her go through the house with you. See if anything's missing."

"Will do." The officer walked away.

"You sure know how to pick 'em, Jake," said Riley when he and Jake were alone. "The man you're hired to find, finds you and ends up dead at your feet. That ever happened before?"

"Never."

"Yeah, well," Riley mused. "Any idea who was with him?"

"None," Jake said, his head pounding.

"Epstein doesn't have much of a description," Riley added. "He said he saw someone running from the house. He told him to stop and was fired upon. Said he looked like a kid. Put some jeans on, some sneakers, and who the hell doesn't look like a kid?"

"He'll show up," Jake said as an officer came out the back door.

"Sergeant? You'd better come up, Sarge."

"What is it?"

"The second-floor game room, sir. It looks like somebody got mad as hell at some photographs."

—13—

Mildreth Gibbon Preston looked down at her hands folded quietly in her lap, then, back at Jake, who was sitting across from her in her Beacon Hill living room. She'd adopted this pose while the police questioned her; it was how she assumed Sergeant Riley expected her to behave—bewildered with a weak, whispery voice. When the police finally left, she strode to the Chippendale sideboard centered against the far wall and opened it.

"I believe a scotch would do nicely," she said and set out two glasses. "Ice?"

"Please," Jake answered.

Mrs. Preston poured, handed Jake his drink, and sat back down. She drank in silence, waiting for the calm she expected to follow. "You knew, didn't you," she said. "You knew someone would be in my house."

Jake nodded. His head felt as though it housed a sloshing water balloon. "It was a good guess," he answered, not admitting he'd guessed wrong.

"But Colin . . ." Her voice trailed off in disbelief. "I feel so sorry for his wife and those three children. It's just horrible." A little more scotch helped. "And you, you let me think I was looking out for Watson when he was looking out for me." Watson was between them, lying on his belly like a black sphinx. "He wouldn't let me out of the car until he knew I was safe."

"He's as good as they come," Jake stated.

Watson knew he was being talked about and curled his tongue

in a self-conscious yawn. Although the words were lost on him, he understood the tone—it was all praise.

"He's got a sixth sense," Jake told her. "When there's trouble, he's there."

"Just like you."

Jake drank half his drink and rattled the ice cubes. "I wasn't much help to Colin Owens. He goes from lost to dead in about two weeks. That's a pretty fast trip."

"I wish I'd never hired him," Mrs. Preston said. "I wish I'd never gotten involved in any of this." She shook her head wearily. "I wish I'd taken Myron's advice and sold out."

The admission surprised Jake. "Sold the land?" he asked.

"That's right. Myron knew of a buyer, a despicable sort of man, so I refused to even consider the offer."

"Who was it?"

Mildreth's expression soured. "Oliver did not like the man's name spoken in this house," she said bitterly.

"You're not inviting him to tea." Jake sounded annoyed. "Who was the buyer?"

Mildreth sipped her scotch tentatively. Oliver's wishes were not promises to cigar-store Indians.

"Mrs. Preston . . ."

"Oh, all right," she snapped. "The man's name is Woodbine. Frazer Woodbine."

The name reverberated in Jake's groggy head. "Woodbine?" he repeated and felt for the card in his shirt pocket.

"Do you know him?"

Jake looked at the card and put it back. "I had an appointment with him a few hours ago, but no, I don't know him."

"To your credit," Mildreth said. "He's a scoundrel, and in your line of work you associate with enough scoundrels." She flipped her hand back and forth, dismissing all thoughts of Frazer Woodbine. "I'll hear no more about it. We'll respect Oliver's wishes and not speak of him in this house. Besides, there's enough on your plate with that mess upstairs. Come on."

Mildreth stood and led the way up the curved stairway to the second-floor billiard room, where nearly a hundred eight-by-ten black and white photographs were ripped to bits. She sighed at the destruction. Jake bent down and picked up the torn print of an aerial flyover.

"You told Sergeant Riley that Colin took these," he said, putting back the scrap.

"That's right."

"When you hired him, did you request a set of prints from his flyover?"

"I did. He said I wouldn't be able to tell much since they were taken from the air, were black and white, and were at some scale or another. I told him I understood but wanted them anyway. I wanted to be a part of every step of my husband's memorial until it was done, and done to my satisfaction. Those were the conditions of Colin's employment. If he didn't like it, he could step aside and I'd hire someone else."

"So he shot the survey and brought you the prints."

"Reluctantly. I used the billiard table to lay them out like a picture puzzle. It wasn't hard," she said with absolute confidence. "Colin said it would be, but I managed. I wanted to look at the place, you understand. I wanted to see all of it."

"Did Colin know you'd done that?" Jake asked.

"Laid them out?"

"Yes."

She nodded. "He did. I phoned him. There appeared to be a problem. Something about the photographs seemed not quite right. In my memory, one of the trails we hiked most went left around a certain majestic stand of pines. Oliver loved the quiet there, so I was looking for the trail, remembering the hikes, reliving the smells. . . ." Her voice flattened. She looked down at her folded hands and took in a breath. "Well, the trail seemed wrong somehow. That's really all I could make sense of. It was just wrong, so I called Mr. Owens to see if he hadn't made some mistake."

"Wrong how?" Jake wanted to know.

"I couldn't say. It's been years since we were up there. After looking at all those photographs, I couldn't be certain of anything. Did the trail go left as I remembered? Or did it go right? I still couldn't say. Besides, the view from an airplane only confused me more."

"What did Owens say when you asked him if he'd made a mistake?"

Mrs. Preston's back stiffened. "He denied it, of course. He said he was a professional and didn't make mistakes. I told him I didn't either and could prove it."

"By comparing the photos Colin took with the ones Oliver had taken years ago," Jake added knowingly.

"That's right."

"How'd Colin react?"

"I don't think he said a thing. I told him when he got his wits about him to call back and we'd set up an appointment to examine the photos together here at my house. The next I'd heard, Colin had disappeared."

Jake sipped more scotch, thinking as the liquid warmed his insides. "That call is the key, Mrs. Preston. Colin was no doubt afraid you'd spotted something in those pictures." The sight of them ripped to shreds was disheartening to say the least. "If only we could compare them ourselves," Jake said. The doorbell interrupted his wishful thinking.

"Could that be the police again?" Mildreth wondered aloud as Jake followed her down the stairs. With each step, she gained more resolve to answer a dozen additional questions of the ever probing Riley.

But it wasn't the police staring back at her when she opened the door. It was Terry Owens. She stared intently at Jake with red-rimmed eyes as Mrs. Preston led her past Watson and into the living room.

"I had to come," Terry said.

"Of course, dear. Of course." Mildreth Preston guided her gently to a club chair.

Jake was at the sideboard and brought Terry back a brandy. She took it without a word, nodded, and put the snifter to her lips. Her face looked pale and lifeless, sapped by the shock of her husband's death.

"How are the children?" Mrs. Preston asked kindly.

"My brother's with them." Her voice quavered and her chin tightened. "I haven't told them."

A nervous silence settled in so heavily that even Watson cowered. Mrs. Owens held the snifter tentatively in both hands.

"Colin was at the house this afternoon," she finally said and turned to Jake. "He and another man came. The other man . . . mean little eyes . . . had a gun."

"Did this other man use a name?"

"No name."

"What'd he look like?" Jake asked. Terry described what might be Kenney Ruggles. Finally, she said, "Colin was being held."

Jake wanted to believe her. "By whom?" he asked gently.

"I don't know. He didn't say, or was afraid to." The sentences were now pouring out. "That's why he never called or tried to make contact. He couldn't. I knew he wouldn't run off and leave us. I knew he'd never do that." The words caught in her throat. The shock and fear of being alone seemed to have gotten the best of her, and she broke into tears.

In an instant, Mildreth Preston was beside her, silently consoling her, holding her close.

"I'm sorry." Terry Owens's voice was grave and pitiful. "I didn't mean . . ."

"Shhhhhhh. It's all right."

"Really, I . . ."

"We'll hear no more about it," Mrs. Preston said as Jake looked on uncomfortably. It was a scene he'd witnessed dozens of times and experienced a time or two. Someone you love is dead. There's no easy way to say it, no easy way to get through it. Someone you love is dead, and it always hurts.

Jake poured himself another drink and waited for Terry Owens to calm down. When the sobbing stopped, he got back to work. "Where was Colin being held?" he asked.

"I don't know."

"He'd been gone two weeks. He must've said something."

Terry's eyes flicked on Jake, then back to her brandy. Staring at the amber liquid, she said, "I can't answer that. I don't know."

"Look, Mrs. Owens . . ."

Mildreth turned on Jake. "Do we have to go on?" she snapped. "The poor girl—"

"No, no, please," Terry said. "I'd like to help."

They exchanged sympathetic smiles then Mrs. Preston went back to her seat.

Terry Owens swallowed a sip of brandy. "I'll be fine," she said, feeling the warmth of the alcohol. "Really. I'll be fine." Her chin jutted out defiantly. She bolstered herself with another swallow of brandy. "Colin needed information," she said.

"About what?" Jake asked.

"This house." Terry glanced at Mrs. Preston, who seemed to stiffen before her eyes. "Colin had to get in."

"That was easy enough," Mildreth stated. "He had an invitation."

"The point is," Jake said to Mrs. Preston, "he didn't want you around. That's right, isn't it, Terry?"

"I don't know," she answered Jake, then glanced falteringly at Milly Preston. Terry looked every bit the betrayer. "I'm sorry," she said to Mildreth. "You don't know how sorry."

"For what?"

"For setting you up," Jake explained as suspicions began to jell. "Colin wanted access to your house so he could examine the photographs. *Both* sets, alone." He turned his attention to Terry Owens. "What do the photographs show?" he asked accusingly. "What's up there on the mountain that Colin didn't want anyone to see?"

"I don't know."

Jake wouldn't let up. "What was your part in this, Terry?" he demanded.

"I had no part," she blurted.

"Of course not. You just showed up here one day. What was the plan? You befriend Mrs. Preston, get to know the house, then switch a picture or two?"

"No!"

"Or just let Colin in when the timing is right?" Jake pressed.

"No! No! No!"

"But Sellers's death made your part unnecessary. With Mildreth away at the funeral, all Colin had to do was waltz in and take his sweet time. Problem was, somebody saw him break in. Trapped, he destroyed the pictures."

"No!"

"Why?" Jake snapped. "What didn't he want anyone to see?"

"I don't know!" Terry shot back as Mildreth leaped to her feet.

"Stop it!" Mrs. Preston stood inches from Jake. "Can't you see that the poor girl is distraught? I won't have you badgering her. Not in my home."

Jake sidestepped Milly Preston and stood in front of Terry. "Do yourself a favor, Mrs. Owens," he pressed on. "You came here to get something out in the open. Now's your chance."

"I can't."

"Of course you can."

She put one hand to her throat and whispered, "Please."

Jake reached for her. "Mrs. Owens . . ."

Her color went ghastly white and her eyes popped wide. "Why? Why did they have to shoot him?"

Jake stepped back, the moment lost. "I don't have the answer," he said.

"But why? Why did they shoot him?" she asked again, catching her breath with jerky sighing sounds that cracked into grotesque sobs. They seemed to come from the very center of her heart.

Mildreth glared at Jake. "I'd like for you to go," she demanded. "Now. This very minute."

"Mrs. Preston . . ."

Her eyes burned. "This very minute, Mr. Eaton, and I mean it!"

Jake put his glass down. He motioned to Watson, who sauntered to his side, seeming keenly aware that things were not right. Jake stepped to the door, opened it, and let Watson lead the way into the sultry early evening air.

Being kicked out of Milly's house, trifling as it was, had an odd effect on Jake. He felt he was moments away from getting something out of Terry Owens when Mildreth Preston—protector of all—stepped in like a referee and stopped the bout. He was frustrated, uneasy, as if wading on the edge of a lagoon while a tidal wave approached.

"Damn," Jake grumbled. He bent down and rubbed Watson's

fine black coat. "You may not know it, pup, but this is one hell of a business we're in. Got any ideas for a career change?"

Watson rolled onto his back and struck at the sky with his sturdy legs.

"Oh, yeah?" Jake scratched Watson's belly, sending the already playful dog into wondrous fits. "What makes you so damn happy?" Jake teased. "Tell me."

"Tell us both."

Jake stopped his conversation with Watson and looked up. Gloria was standing beside him, her expression serious.

"Too bad he can't," she said, forcing a smile.

Jake stood, brushing pieces of grass from his chinos. "Not that I'm not delighted, but what brings you here?"

"I could say I was in the neighborhood."

"You could."

"Wouldn't believe me?"

"Don't think so."

The slight shrug of her shoulders seemed to relax her, make her somehow more lovely. She managed a genuine smile this time, and Jake kissed her lightly on the lips. "I'm glad to see you," he said.

Watson sat up. Gloria scruffed him along the neck. "I'm glad to see you both," she said.

"How'd you find us?"

"A shooting on Beacon Hill at one of the finest addresses is all over the news. I happened to be watching." It seemed an embarrassing admission. "I had to come." She looked at Jake lovingly. "The reporter said an unidentified man had been killed. I thought that unidentified man was you." She could barely get the words out, they hurt so much.

Jake put his arms around her and held her tight. For the longest time, he could think of nothing to say, no great line to knock back her fear. Finally, he realized there wasn't one.

"Come on," he said. "Let's go find us a drink."

—14—

The Hampshire House was a second-floor bar and restaurant on Beacon Street overlooking the Public Garden not five blocks from Mildreth Gibbon Preston's home. Jake parked his car, let Watson watch the world go by from the driver's seat, and escorted Gloria up the front stairs and into the bar. They took a booth in the corner and ordered. When the waiter brought the drinks, Gloria thanked Jake.

"For what?"

"For not getting yourself hurt."

"Gloria . . ."

"I know, I know, it goes with the job. Still, seeing Milly's house on the TV screen and that reporter speaking into the microphone without the slightest hint in her voice that she felt anything. . . . They were just words to her. Somebody had been killed a few feet away from where she stood, and all that mattered was that her hair was perfect and the words caught enough of the drama."

"It was a fluke," Jake said.

"Tell that to the unidentified man. Did he have a family?"

"He did," Jake told her. "A wife and three kids." He watched as Gloria looked stunned. "Don't ask if—"

". . . If I don't want the answer." She nodded, understanding. "I know. I was just thinking—"

"Don't. The past is past. Leave it there."

Gloria turned her glass in circles, lifted it, and sipped. "They make a good gimlet here."

"They do."

"Not as good as mine."

"No. Not that good."

There was a long, uneasy silence. "What was the man's name?" she asked, looking down into her cocktail.

Jake didn't hesitate. Life jumps ahead, sometimes dragging you along, sometimes running over you. Either way, life goes bumping along. "His name was Colin Owens," he said, annoyed.

"My God," Gloria gasped. She looked steadily at Jake, troubled by his expression. "What's the matter?" she asked.

"The matter is, I've been a stupid ass," Jake said, annoyed. "This started out as a simple little case, and once I get to New Hampshire, I can't see the forest for the trees." Jake sipped his drink. "I should've been at Milly's house waiting for Colin. Photographs have been staring me in the face from the beginning and I can't make out the image. I've been blind, Gloria. Stupid, blind, and— now—pissed off."

Jake drank more of his gimlet, then slid his arm across the table and took Gloria's hand in his. He put his other hand on top and cradled hers.

"Sorry," he said. "Sorry for the outburst and sorry you're close to this. I thought when I took Milly's case, you might have an interest, but now I don't think that's such a good idea. You should stay away."

"Hide, you mean?"

"No. Stay away."

"My father wouldn't approve."

Jake's temper was short, and he snapped, "How would you know? You haven't said more than two words to him in months."

"I called him."

"You called him?" Jake felt like cowering in a corner. It had been his suggestion that she call, and he wanted to be happy for her, but his voice echoed his surprise, and he knew it. "You called him," he said, tenderly squeezing her hand.

Gloria studied the caring in his eyes. "We had a drink together," she said, smiling slightly. "You knew I would. I didn't know it, but you did."

"A lucky guess."

"You can pass it off as that if you want."

Jake's finger traced Gloria's soft palm. "All right. Let's say that I wanted you to. Let's say every spare moment, I sent you vibes."

"They took." She lifted her gimlet and drank. "At least partly."

Jake leaned against the soft leather backrest. "Which part?"

"The conversation with my father. Every time we have one, I'm reminded what a remarkable man he is."

"The same could be said for the daughter," Jake added.

"I believed that once, Jake. Now I'm not so sure." She poked absently at an ice cube with her finger. "My father used to take me to Red Sox games and point out the great hitters."

"Ted Williams."

Gloria smiled. "Before my time. I was thinking more of Yaz. When Yaz was in a slump, my father used to say that the great hitters never lose their confidence. They get lazy or lose their concentration, but they never lose their confidence. They always believe that the very next pitch is the one going over the wall."

"Sometimes it is," Jake said.

"And sometimes it isn't."

"You still have to stand in the box and swing. You're not out until the third strike."

"I tell myself that. Once in a while, I even get myself to believe it. But the fact remains, Jake, I've lost . . . no, 'lost' isn't the right word. I didn't lose my confidence, I had it ripped away. Stolen right out from under my very eyes."

Jake kept his gaze on her but said nothing.

"You don't understand, do you?" Gloria asked.

"I'm trying."

"No, Jake, *I'm* trying." Her voice was up and edgy. "A man on Nantucket threatens to kill me. He stalks me, teases me, hunts me down—"

"I stopped him." Jake's voice carried the same edge.

"I know that. You . . . *you* stopped him. That's what's hard. I couldn't do it myself. But, in one sense, a man like that can never be stopped. The threat itself does a certain amount of damage." Her eyes looked right through Jake.

"When I was at Harvard," she continued, "I had a small apartment in Cambridge. An elderly woman lived on the second floor. A very nice lady. Retired. Read a lot. Went shopping and generally stayed around the building. One day, two men followed her into the foyer and stole her pocketbook. She never trusted anyone after that. Never greeted me with the same smile, the same warmth. I couldn't understand what a simple thing like stealing a pocketbook had done to that poor woman. I was so naive, I went out and bought her a new one. I knocked on her door and held it before her. 'Miss Cartwright,' I said, 'I know you've lost your pocketbook, so I picked you up a new one.' She stared blankly at me for the longest time, as if I wasn't really there. Finally she closed the door in my face."

"Without taking the gift?"

"That's the point, Jake. The men stole her peace of mind, her view of the world, her ability to live in it. I was only giving back a handbag."

"What happened to the lady?"

Gloria used her fingers to comb back the hair that had fallen across her eyes. "Six months later she moved away."

Jake wasn't sympathetic. "Meaning she gave up."

Gloria looked hurt. "That's the simple way of putting it. And I imagine you—and to some degree my father—see me in the same terms. I've given up."

Jake didn't jump in with an apology. Instead, he said, "I'm not judging you, Gloria. It may sound like it, but I'm not."

"I think you are."

"Then you're wrong."

"Just like that. All cut and dried."

"Not cut and dried at all." Jake turned the glass in his hand and took a long breath. "Look, I don't want to argue. I did enough of that when I was married."

"What do you want to do?"

"I'm asking myself that same question." He took another drink to wet his dry throat. "I don't have all the answers, just enough to stay alive in the business I'm in. The rest of it is as iffy and confusing and unclear for me as it appears to be for you. The big difference is I'm trying to figure how you might fit into my life, and you're trying to figure what kind of life you've been left with. All I know is the man who threatened you is dead. I killed him."

Gloria squirmed at the memory. "I don't want to think about it."

"Apparently you do. You've been thinking about it every day at the exclusion of everything else."

"Stop it."

"And those are big issues you've been thinking about. Life and death. What are you going to do with your future? The big issues. Whoever said 'the little things bring you down, the big ones take care of themselves' didn't know what the hell he was talking about. If you don't know how you want to live your life, you end up like Miss Cartwright. Lost."

"I'm afraid I am lost, Jake."

Jake's voice shot up. "No, you're not." He looked around self-consciously and lowered his voice. "You're Gloria Gorham. You're bright. You're talented. You might be standing in the batter's box with two strikes, but you can damn well swing and hit the next one out of the park."

A slight smile brightened her expression. "I'd like to believe that."

"You should."

"Why?"

"Because it's true. You met with your father. A quitter wouldn't have made the effort."

"It wasn't much."

"Measure the step by its direction, not by how long it was. All I know is, I'm very happy you took it."

He raised his glass in salute. Gloria lifted hers and they clicked.

"Maybe it was a start," she admitted. She set down her gimlet and took Jake's hand. "You're a remarkable man."

"Me and your father. Now you've got two in your life," he teased.

But the moment didn't last, and he was back to business.

"What did F. Gordon have to say about the surveyor he recommended to Oliver Preston?"

Gloria looked solemnly at Jake. "It doesn't matter now," she said. "The man's dead."

Jake felt the name catch in his throat. "Colin Owens?"

"Afraid so."

"Damn."

—15—

"Colin Owens is what?"

"Dead."

Jake was in his apartment picking up a few clean turtlenecks and his .44 Magnum. The .38 was fine for everyday use, but for special occasions Jake hauled out the artillery. Something told him that the next trip to Winslow would require it. While Watson snacked on the leftovers brought back from Jake and Gloria's wonderful French dinner at DuBarry's, Jake packed and put in a call to Lieutenant Moreau.

"Owens broke into Mildreth Preston's home. A cop shot him making a run for it. From Terry Owens's description, it sounds like Kenney Ruggles was with him."

"I knew that kid was no good the first time I saw him."

"He may be proving you right, Lieutenant."

"We'll find out when I pick him up."

"Hold off on that, Lieutenant."

"Hold off?"

"Kenney might be the Winslow link we're looking for. If you bust him, we may never get to the bottom of Sellers's murder."

"Yeah, well, I'm already at the bottom of it." Moreau let the moment build, to Jake's consternation. "Slocum and I searched the rest of the office and came up with a deposit slip for a bank in Boston. Sellers deposited ten thousand dollars two days before he was killed."

"Quite a haul for a part-time job."

"Just what we were thinking."

"I don't suppose enough money goes through that office for him to have been skimming."

"Not even close."

"So who paid off Sellers and why?" Jake thought aloud.

"At least we're asking the same questions."

"You got any answers, Lieutenant?"

"Not yet."

"How about the check on that license plate I asked you to run?"

"Computer's down over in Concord. Should have it later today," Moreau said. Then he added, "Be nice to know how much is in that account."

"My thoughts exactly." Jake asked for the account number and the name of the bank. "Bankers worry more about privacy suits than anything else nowadays. I'll run this through a friend of mine, see what he comes up with."

"Hope you do better than I did. By the way, last night I spoke to Myron's wife, Cora Sellers. She didn't know a thing about the money. Said she'd never heard of Harbor National Bank."

"Do you believe her?"

"No reason not to."

Jake could think of ten thousand reasons. "I'll see what I can find out. And Lieutenant?"

"Yeah?"

"Don't try anything foolish with Kenney Ruggles. There's no telling what he's into or what he might be willing to do to get out. Stay on your toes," Jake warned. "You and Slocum both."

"Thanks, Eaton. We'll stay out of trouble."

"Good," Jake said, wondering if that were possible. Something told him it wasn't as he hung up.

Jake's friend at The Gorham Corporation was Lewis Metcalf, a corporate attorney workaholic. When Jake called his home, Mrs. Metcalf said what she often said: "Try the office."

Jake poured Watson a small bowl of red wine to go along with the crepe. He set it on the floor and patted his partner.

"Refinements," Jake said to the pup. "Remember who our client is, boy. Mildreth Preston. Check that. Mildreth *Gibbon* Preston."

Watson hesitated, stuck his tongue in the wine, and just as quickly removed it. His eyes cut Jake a questioning look.

Jake patted him again. "I think you're right," Jake said. "I know '93 isn't a good vintage, but it'll grow on you."

Jake left the bowl on the floor and Watson behind to enjoy it. He got his keys to The Gorham Corporation's forty-plus stories of polished granite and sparkling glass on the edge of Boston's financial district and headed into the city. Lewis had a corner office overlooking the harbor and Logan Airport. On clear nights, such as tonight, planes stacked in their holding patterns looked like fireflies circling right outside the window.

Jake announced himself on the intercom and entered the office. "Nice view," Jake noted.

"So I'm told," Lewis replied with a smile. Lewis was sixty, trim, and fit. The only thing that pried him from his office was an occasional jog and any game necessitating a racket, most often squash in spring and tennis in fall.

Jake pulled out a chair and sat. "You work too hard, Lewis."

"As if this were a social call." Lewis put down his pen. "How's Watson?"

"Vigilant as ever."

"And yourself?"

"No complaints."

"Who listens anyway, right?" He raised his right arm and pointed. "Tennis elbow is my latest. It's the damnedest thing. No forehand at all."

"Probably old age."

"So my wife tells me. But I'm not dead yet and don't intend to consider it for quite some time. Now, what is it with this account you called about?"

"It's tied up in a murder investigation."

"Whose?"

"A sheriff in Winslow, New Hampshire."

Lewis brightened. "Ah, so that's the connection. I read about that in the paper but didn't know it was your case."

"It isn't. I was looking for a surveyor who disappeared. He's dead, too—shot this afternoon running down an alley."

A flash of recognition spread across Lewis's face. "The one caught robbing Mildreth Gibbon Preston's place," he said.

"You know her?"

"Who doesn't. Mildreth is—shall we say—a fixture, and I don't mean that unkindly. She's big-hearted and has the pocketbook to be generous. It's a good combination."

"Then you heard about her land giveaway?"

"More than heard about it. Gloria called to get my opinion when Mildreth first thought up the idea." Lewis raised his hands and brought the tips of his fingers to his eyelids. He rubbed the tiredness from each eye. "Terrible business what's happened to Gloria. I encouraged her to stay involved with Milly's memorial."

"So did I," Jake said disappointedly.

Lewis read Jake's tone. "You think that was a bad idea?" he asked.

"I do now, and I've told her so."

"Well, all I know is she has to get active in life again." He put his hands down. "She's got to get interested in something other than that old boat. Oliver's memorial was an idea, perhaps not a good one."

"I couldn't agree more, Lewis, but—"

"But you're not here to talk about that."

"No, I'm not, but you just reminded me of something. Gloria said that Oliver Preston once worked for The Gorham Corporation."

"That's right. He was a consultant on retainer, much the same as you are."

"Doing what?"

"Collecting information. You have to remember that this was years before the Environmental Protection Agency had been created. There was no Clean Air Act, no Clean Water Act. Oh, there were rumblings that the federal government was about to pass something, but no one took them seriously. The truth is, at first, no one took Oliver Preston seriously either. Or, if they did, they didn't admit it. No one except Gloria's father."

"She said they had a tremendous respect for each other."

"Respect and, over the years, friendship. You might say this corporation brought two very interesting minds together. Oliver believed that if the environmental movement was to survive, the public focus couldn't remain on the occasional oil spill washing up on the beaches. It makes good headlines but is forgotten in days. No, Oliver wanted changes made from the ground up. What all of us do with half-used paint cans and oil from our cars is where the long-term battle has to be waged. All of us, according to Oliver, including big business. At that time, most businesses didn't want anything to do with him. Few had environmental issues as a priority. They cut into profits, so to hell with it. All except F. Gordon. He opened the front door for Oliver and gave him free rein."

"To do what?"

"Study, monitor, measure, and report on what The Gorham Corporation used, discarded, recycled, wasted—whatever. At that time, GC had interests in everything from mining operations to building offshore drill rigs. Oliver and his team spent nearly a year researching and writing their findings. They used the data he collected as the basis for his confrontation with that idle-brained congressman who tried to shut up Oliver during one of the hearings held in Washington. 'We can't change the world, Dr. Preston,' the old fool said. Replied Oliver, 'Congressman, we already have.'"

Lewis smiled warmly. "That was a very proud moment—not only for Oliver Preston, but also for this company. As I've told you before, Jake, there aren't many companies with a conscience, but The Gorham Corporation is one, and one of the best."

Jake had heard it before and believed it. "Or you wouldn't be working here," he said.

"Correct, and neither would you. Be honest. You'd have nothing to do with us if we were another Woodbine."

Jake looked as if he'd just learned of forbidden fruit.

"Name ring a bell?" Lewis asked.

Jake nodded. "I had an appointment with him this afternoon. Missed it."

"You missed it, all right," Lewis told him. "Otis Woodbine's been dead for years. His company's long out of business."

Jake shook his head. "Wrong name. The man I was to meet is Frazer. His company's in business and is called ChemTrol."

"You're a generation off. Frazer Woodbine is the son."

"So? Fill me in on daddy."

"Calling Otis Woodbine 'daddy' makes him sound almost human," Lewis said bluntly. "The man took advantage of everything and everyone he could. Oliver Preston exposed him for what he was."

"And what was he?" Jake wanted to know.

"An ingrate. A man without a conscience. King of the midnight haulers." Lewis reached up and touched the tip of his burning ears. "Sorry," he said. "Very unlawyerly."

Jake flicked a restrained smile. "Why's he bother you?" he asked.

"Because Otis Woodbine and GC once did business. We didn't know he was a toxic dumper at the time. Still, the fact remains, some of GC's waste ended up poured down some illegal hole. F. Gordon was horrified."

"How'd you discover it?"

"We didn't. Oliver found the discrepancy in his audit."

"Walk me through it," Jake said.

"Not much to it, really. Woodbine was in the waste removal business. He'd bring a tanker truck to one of our plants, pick up the chemical waste, and haul it to one of his disposal sites. At the end of the month, we'd get a hauler's manifest showing what and how much was treated, which site it went to, and which of our plants it came from. Each of our plants also kept records. Cross-checking those, Oliver spotted a problem. One of our plants shipped six truckloads of benzene—a commonly used solvent—through Woodbine, but only four were ever signed for at the disposal end."

"A mistake?"

"The first time it happened, we thought so. The second and third time it happened, we knew we had a problem. Oliver found other companies where the same thing was going on. Woodbine was farming out some of each shipment to moonlighters."

"When was this?" Jake asked.

Lewis thought a moment. "Twenty, twenty-five years ago. About the time Otis Woodbine went out of business."

"He go broke?"

"Far from it. Rumor had it he made millions illegally dumping. When the authorities got involved, Woodbine declared bankruptcy and left the spoils for others to clean up. From what I understand, his son, Frazer, has tried to do some of that."

"Clean up the sins of the father?"

"To some degree."

"You don't sound convinced," Jake commented.

"I'm not. Mind you, I don't have any proof, but I don't trust the son any more than I trusted the father. But I will say one thing, even if Frazer isn't cleaning up his father's mistakes, he is cleaning up his act. Frazer's sharp. He learned from every mistake his father made, even to the point of setting up ChemTrol like a hydra, with dozens of wholly-owned subsidiaries beneath it. If you cut the head off one, others with names like EarthFine, Filter-Clean, ChemClean, and more pop up."

"That doesn't make him illegal," Jake reminded him.

"No," Lewis admitted. "It makes him what he is, Otis Woodbine's son. If you want my opinion, be damn careful when you're around him."

"Eyes are wide open, Lewis."

"The point is to keep them open so you can live to a ripe old age and come down with tennis elbow like me. Now, didn't you come to see me about some bank account?"

"That's right. Nothing fancy. A little private inquiry. Whose name is it in, how much is on account, that sort of thing." Jake handed Lewis the account number.

"ASAP, I assume."

"Correct."

Lewis glanced at the number and the name of the bank. "You'll have it first thing in the morning. I have an old friend at Harbor National who knows how to be discreet."

Jake looked at his watch. It was just past midnight. "It is the morning," he said. "Care to join me for a nightcap?"

"Love one."

"It's on me."

"Fine. You pay and I won't make my usual pitch to get you to join us here full-time."

"I've got a job, Lewis."

"I know, but GC needs you. We'd set you up with a nice office, a wonderful view, more clients than—"

Jake waited at the door for Lewis to put on his suit coat. "Not the usual pitch, huh?"

"I won't say another word."

"Promise?"

They stepped out into the hall and walked along toward the elevator in silence.

"Long day," Jake said finally.

Lewis pushed the "down" button. "Very," he said as the door opened and they got in.

—16—

Early the next morning, Jake tossed his bag in the back of the car and by nine o'clock was well into the mountains and the tall pines of New Hampshire. It was a beautiful morning—bright, clear, and springtime cold. The ponds still carried a thin skin of ice, but the streams ran fast with melted snow.

At a small diner where Jake stopped for coffee, he followed Watson for a short walk along a path snaking between huge granite boulders. The air was sharp, the scent from the pine trees fresh and untainted. Jake sat on a sun-warmed boulder while Watson sniffed his way toward the edge of a crooked stream. It roared as it plunged over a high spillway and cascaded down the rocks, slick and smooth from the force of the water. Jake stood mesmerized by the beauty and haunted by one thought: Why would somebody want to poison the stream on Milly Preston's land?

Watson thrust a foot into the frigid water and quickly pulled it back. A few yards ahead was a wooden bridge. The dog ambled across while Jake went back up the trail to the parking lot and the pay phone. He punched in his credit card number and Lewis Metcalf's private line.

Lewis was waiting for him with a bombshell. "It's a joint account, Jake, shared by one Myron W. Sellers and Colin D. Owens. The current balance is four hundred thousand."

The hair prickled on Jake's neck. "Jesus."

Lewis continued. "My contact at the bank is checking on this, but a preliminary look indicates deposits every few months."

"A payoff?"

"It would seem so."

But for what? Jake wondered. "Who opened the account?"

"I don't have that yet. Even my friend needs a little more time. Anything else you'd like him to dig up?"

"Yeah. When it was opened might come in handy."

"You got it," Lewis said. "Where should I contact you?"

"The inn. And thanks, Lewis."

"Anytime," Lewis said.

Jake hung up just as Watson—wide eyed, wet, and out of breath—trotted up.

"Took the plunge anyway, huh?"

Watson looked contented even though he would have to ride in the back, where wet dogs always rode.

"Sure," Jake said, as if Watson had just asked why Jake hadn't swum with him. "Soon as I find out where the four hundred thousand came from. You got any ideas?"

Watson shook.

"You're a big help," Jake said and made another call. This one was to the home of Myron Sellers, about an hour up the highway.

Jake made his appointment, then climbed into his car and followed the old man's directions. He was preoccupied by an account with four hundred thousand in it. Who in Winslow would be throwing around that kind of money? he wondered as he turned off on a narrow blacktop, then swung immediately into an unpaved drive. Sellers's house sat back from the road on a hill surrounded by mature maples and pines and clumps of birch. The grounds were clean, the grass brown and dewy.

The house itself was as simple and plain as a box. The screened front porch was furnished with white Adirondack lawn chairs. The shades were drawn, but Jake could see someone move behind a screen door. He pulled up beside Sellers's police car, got out, ascended the porch steps, and knocked.

The man who opened the door was small and bent, as if all the wrinkles on his graying face had somehow pulled him forward. Holding a cigarette between tobacco-stained fingers, he blew smoke, coughed, then looked at Jake by turning himself to one side.

"You the fella who called?" The voice was thin and dry.

"I am." Jake spoke louder than usual, thinking the old man deaf.

"Come in."

Cakes, pies, and casseroles were crowded on tables, as were full grocery bags and stacks of clean dishes. The villagers had honored the deceased and made life easier for the living.

"You're who?" stammered the old man, his false teeth clicking. "Fambly?"

Deaf and blind, thought Jake and shook his head. "A friend."

"Ohhhhhhh." It was clear that he didn't understand.

"Where's Mrs. Sellers?"

"Who? Mrs. . . . ?" Then a hint of recognition. "Oh, my daughter, ya know."

Jake cracked a how-about-that smile. "Where is she?"

The old man waved in the direction of the doorway. "Livin' room." Smoke rolled from his nose as he inhaled the last of his cigarette. He put it out, then rattled another cough. "She needs comp'ny. Understandable, I guess. Me, I'd just as soon be left alone," he said and pulled a bag and papers from his shirt pocket. He tapped the tobacco deftly on the paper and rolled a perfect smoke. He popped one end of it in his mouth and lowered himself into a chair. "You know Myron?" he asked, lighting up.

"Not well," Jake said.

"Didn't miss nothin'," the old man told him. "He was a sonofabitch I planned on shootin' myself."

Jake stared at the old man. Crazy? he wondered.

"Don't look so surprised. If my daughter had any backbone, she'd a done it. Somebody saved us both the trouble, and I know who," he said with a wheeze.

Jake arched his brows. "You do?" he asked incredulously.

"I said it, didn't I?" the old man spit out. "I know who done it. Damn right, I do."

Jake nodded. "I'll bite," he said. "Who?"

The old man shook his head. "Won't say. I don't like that sonofabitch none either, but I know him better'n I know you."

Not too likable yourself, Jake thought as he entered the living room. Cora Sellers sat rubbing her red puffy eyes. From what Jake knew about Myron, Cora looked like the sort of woman he would have been drawn to. She had a gentle, warm expression that even sadness couldn't completely hide.

"Mrs. Sellers? It's not much comfort, I know, but I am sorry about your husband," Jake said.

She smiled appreciatively, not looking up from her folded hands. "Kind of you." She paused. "Is dad smoking again?"

"Makes a fine roll-your-own."

"Wish he wouldn't. He's been told, you know. Warned is more like it. Stop or you'll die. I'd call that a warning. But he's stubborn. Part mule, I guess."

"Used to smoke myself," Jake said and felt foolish at how awkward it was saying anything in moments like this. Words seemed to hang meaningless in the air.

"You had the good sense to quit. Dad won't. Then he tries to hide how much he smokes by making his own. But I know—I can count. And I know he's killing himself right in front of me." She looked past Jake. "I'm glad you called first," she said unconvincingly. "Too many people just stop by—as if I want a house full of neighbors." She looked seriously at Jake for the first time. "You're the detective."

"That's right."

"Lieutenant Moreau mentioned you. I told him everything I knew. I don't know any more."

"What about your father?" Jake asked.

"Dad?"

"He says he knows who did it."

"Dad says whatever flies through his mind. I wouldn't pay him any attention."

"He also said somebody did you and him a favor."

She was quietly pensive.

"Did somebody do you a favor by killing your husband?" Jake asked as Cora Sellers's eyes went back to her hands and stayed there. After a pause, Jake said, "He wouldn't have it wrong, would he? Your dad?"

"I don't know what you're asking," she said unevenly, her hands working.

"Did you kill your husband?"

Her eyes came up. "No. Of course I didn't."

"Money can be a powerful motive. A large sum makes people do very strange things."

She said nothing.

"Did you know your husband died a very wealthy man?" Jake asked into her weary eyes. "I know about the Boston bank and the joint account with Colin Owens."

Slowly she pushed herself up from her chair and walked to the window. From the porch, the old man broke into another coughing fit. "He'll fall asleep in bed is what he'll do. I know it. I've dreamed about it. He'll fall asleep in bed and burn himself up and the house down. Maybe it's just as well," she said and turned back to Jake. "I knew about the money, if that's what you're asking. I never took a penny of it."

"But you knew how much was there."

"I didn't ask. Never did. I knew it was wrong—said so to Myron. Spoke my mind, that's all I could do."

"Mrs. Sellers—"

"We grew up poor. Just like most folks in the village. You know what you haven't got. All you have to do is open your eyes. Most folks don't try to hide it. Being without is nothing to be ashamed of. It's a fact, that's all. The will of God, some say. If you stay in this village, you'll be a poor man the rest of your life and that will never change." She settled in her chair. "What changes is the man."

"You're talking about your husband?"

"I'm talking about Myron Sellers," she said coolly. "I don't know much about the man, really. But he was my husband. Yes, he was." She paused and looked down at the wadded tissues her fingers were twisting. "That's terrible, isn't it? But it's true. Up here with these long winters. People lock themselves inside no better than bears. After a while, Myron never came out. The same could be said of me, I suppose. Pretty soon, both of us were hidden away right inside the same house, just like bears. You don't learn much about a man that way, and what you do learn, you sometimes wish you hadn't."

She's describing the last years of my own marriage, Jake

thought, recalling the depression and the series of incredibly bad, unbearable days. Jake's heart went out to the woman across from him, but he had to continue. "How'd your husband make the money, Mrs. Sellers?" he asked.

"Listening to Colin," she said. "He'd long since stopped paying attention to me. To hear Myron tell it, Colin was a genius. But he wasn't any genius. He was a fool just like my husband." She gazed at Jake. "D'you know what a fool is? A man who can't live with who he is. That's what a fool is."

"What were they doing, Mrs. Sellers? How'd they come up with that kind of money?"

"What most folks do up here. Scratching out a living. If you can't make money, you find ways to save it."

"Pretty hard to scratch out four hundred thousand dollars."

"The amount doesn't matter." She was glaring at Jake, her hot eyes boring through him. "You have to understand that the amount means nothing. The pot of gold was on the path, but it was the wrong path. It was a path traveled by the wicked."

Jake didn't push her. "I'm only trying to help, Mrs. Sellers. Don't you want to find out who killed your husband?"

"I know who killed him," she said wearily. "He didn't pull the trigger, but Colin killed him when he came to Winslow and filled that man's head with dreams." She hesitated and wiped her eyes. "Some men can't live with dreams, Mr. Eaton. It's like a poison; when it runs its course, we bury them."

Poison, Jake thought. "Your husband kept some newspaper clippings in his office about toxic waste dumping that happened around here years ago."

"So?"

"So I was wondering if he could have been involved somehow."

"He was involved," Mrs. Sellers said. "He made the arrests."

"I was thinking of involvement in another way. Involvement of some kind that might explain how he died wealthy."

Mrs. Sellers looked away.

"He was involved, wasn't he?" Jake asked.

"I don't know."

"Mrs. Sellers. Please."

"Ask Colin," she answered tersely.

"He's dead." Jake looked at her in silence. "Colin Owens has been killed," he repeated.

"I can't say I'm sorry," she said. "How? How'd he die?"

"He was shot breaking into Mildreth Preston's home."

A greater sadness crept across her face. "It makes you wonder, doesn't it? What kind of life must they have had together that she wants to build a memorial to her husband? Could Myron and I have missed that much in our married lives?"

Just then the old man maneuvered a turn and wheezed around the corner.

"Hey!" he shouted accusingly at Jake. "You ain't fambly!"

"No, he's not, Papa. He's the private detective who phoned earlier. Remember?" She was speaking as if to a child.

"The detective?"

"That's right."

The old man flicked a knobby hand toward Jake. "You need any help, I'm your man. Joey Barns ain't gonna come easy an' Joey Barns done it."

"Papa, don't say that," she scolded.

"I know what I know."

Cora snapped, "You don't know anything of the kind."

"Been in jail, ain't he? Where do ya think an ornery basta'd like that learns ta be meaner? In jail, that's where. Two years fer burgl'ry, an' it's the damn truth!"

To Jake she said, "Pap thinks Joey Barns committed every crime in the state."

"He shot Myron, didn't he?" the old man struck back.

"Stop it," she warned.

"Soon as I heard about it, I saw it like a dream." The old man turned to Jake. "You'll hav'ta beat a confession outa him, but Joey'll talk."

"That's enough! Pap, stop it!"

The old man jerked his head knowingly to the ceiling. "I suppose he never broke inta my house neither."

"Pap was in Florida a few winters ago, and Joey broke into his house," Cora explained.

"An' a zillion others!"

"And a few others," she corrected. "Myron eventually put a stop to it."

"Myron was such a stupid sonofabitch," the old man snarled.

"Leave it alone, Pap!" she scolded. "He's not yet settled in his grave."

"Bah!"

"I mean it!" she snapped, their eyes locking.

Slowly the old man slipped a cigarette he'd already rolled from his shirt pocket, popped an end of it in his mouth, and lit it. He inhaled deeply, letting the smoke put up a cloud behind his words. "Myron an' Joey Barns was in cahoots," he said.

Cora Sellers bolted to her feet. "I've had enough!"

The old man coughed so deeply his bones rattled. Still he spit out, "Ask anybody. Ask me! My stupid sonofabitchin' son-in-law an' Joey Barns was partners, an' Joey finally done the right thing an' killed him!"

Jake rose with the smoke and the anger. The old man coughed on while Cora—the fight gone from her—impassively looked at her father.

At the car, Jake gazed back toward the house and the suffering that festered and burned there. Myron, he thought, must have coaxed and tended well enough to keep the lid on, but now that he was gone, Cora and the old man hissed like cats.

"Hell of a way to spend your life," Jake said and sat beside Watson, who was now dry enough to ride in the front seat. Jake turned the key, fired the engine, and drove slowly out the road toward Winslow and Joey Barns.

—17—

For as long as anyone could remember, there has always been a Barns fixing engines in Winslow. J. D. Barns started the garage. When he retired Joey took over, but he didn't run the business with the same sense of care and accomplishment his father had before him. J. D. found hours of satisfaction solving the riddle of mechanical failure and firing an engine back to life. Joey—a tall, well-built man with pale blue eyes, a narrow face, and a mean smile—found little satisfaction in anything legal.

As Joey saw it, legal meant a life in Winslow, and the only way out was in a stolen car. So, at thirteen, he hot-wired his first. At fourteen, he did the same four times. He has never looked back except for an occasional stint behind bars, which was almost always shortened because the judge got fooled by Joey's baby face. But people who knew Joey were not fooled. Joey Barns was mean and restless, biting off life in chunks too large for him to chew.

Jake and Watson pulled off the paved road and into the gravel parking lot of the garage—a large, high rectangle of corrugated tin on the sides and a wooden front with Winslow's Engine Repair and Service painted above the door. The sign in the window announcing that the shop would reopen after Myron's funeral was crossed out, with "Closed Temporarily" written below.

Jake stepped from the car and motioned for Watson to follow as he walked to the sliding double doors and tried to open them. They were locked. Around the side he found an entrance to the office. The door was closed but unlocked.

"Stay put," he told Watson and went in.

The office was small and unkempt with a metal desk and chair. Behind the desk were bookshelves filled with various repair manuals and catalogs covered with a mechanic's grease and grime.

Past the filing cabinet was another door that led to the repair bays. Jake could hear cackling voices coming from that direction. He pulled out his .44 Magnum and listened at the door to laughter and a voice he recognized. Slowly, he looked through the glass pane at two angular shadows of men standing near the far mechanic's bay. He quietly opened the door, stepped through, and circled the two with careful side steps. When he was behind them, he raised the revolver to eye level.

"Afraid I'm going to have to interrupt, gentlemen," Jake said as both spun around, eyes as wide as a gazelle's. "Not another step." Jake moved easily around a pile of wrecked car fenders, under a partially dismantled engine hanging from a hoist, and up to a makeshift table cluttered with empty beer and liquor bottles. He picked up a half-empty rum bottle. "A little party?"

"Who the hell are you?"

"He's the cop I told you about," Kenney Ruggles said sharply.

"Private," Jake said and tossed the bottle to Kenney, who barely caught it. "Aren't you going to introduce us?" Jake taunted.

Kenney rocked from side to side, mixing the lack of sleep and booze into more confusion.

"I'm Jake Eaton," Jake said deliberately. "You must be Joey Barns."

"I don't hav'ta say nothin'," Barns snapped, then turned to Kenney. "I told ya ta lock the fuckin' doors!"

"I thought I did."

"Then how the hell'd he get in here?"

"Magic."

Joey glared. "Get the fuck out, man. The same way ya came in, understand?"

"Why make it difficult?"

"You ain't movin'."

"Got something to hide?" Jake pressed.

"I don't talk ta nobody with a gun pointin' at me. I ain't done nothin' an' I ain't sayin' nothin'. Period."

Jake holstered the .44 and stepped closer to Barns.

"My, my," Joey said in mock amazement. "He does simple tricks." Joey was in the middle of a cocky smile when Jake decked him with a stinging right.

With his left hand, Jake reached down and jerked Barns to his feet, slamming him headfirst against the makeshift table. Bottles flew across the floor. Barns struggled for his balance, turned, and looped a right. Jake caught Joey's arm and twisted it into an arm-lock that ripped Joey's jacket at the shoulder.

"All right, all right, Jesus, man!" It was the voice of surrender, but Jake didn't let up.

"I want answers," Jake said evenly.

"I said all right! Come on!"

Jake applied more pressure, then let go. Joey worked on the pain while Jake asked Kenney where he was yesterday afternoon.

"At the funeral."

"After that?"

"Who knows?" Kenney was riding bravado, looking for his stride.

"I do. You were breaking into a house on Beacon Hill."

"Bullshit," Barns said, still rubbing his shoulder.

"From what I hear, he had a good teacher in you, Joey. You did a little time for breaking and entering. Pass on your tricks to Kenney, did you?"

"Where'd ya dig that up?"

"Around."

"Well, bury it. It's like Kenney said, me and him went ta the funeral."

"That a fact."

"It is. Ain't it, Kenney?" Barns's voice was an equal amount of coaxing and reassurance.

Kenney seemed offended. "Get off it, Joey. You heard what I said, didn't ya?" He turned to Jake with a heightened sense of purpose. "We went ta show our respects. That's all we did."

"Never drove to Boston with Colin Owens?"

Kenney's cheeks flushed slightly red. "Don't know anybody named Owens," he said.

"No?"

"No."

"He's dead, Kenney," Jake said evenly. "Shot down coming out of Mildreth Preston's house."

Kenney's face burned a deep red.

"I . . . said . . . I . . . ," Kenney stammered.

Joey put his sore arm around the boy and said to Jake, "Lighten up, will ya? It's like we said. First we went ta the funeral, then some of the fellas who knew Myron came back here for a little celebration. You know, sort of a wake for the old guy. We musta forgot what time it was is all. Partied all night. Right, Kenney?"

"Damn right," Kenney agreed. "We partied all night."

Jake bought none of it. "What'd you do with the gun, Kenney?" he asked.

Kenney looked surprised. "I don't have no gun."

"You can do better than that," Jake teased. "Everybody up here in the sticks has a gun. Maybe you never pulled the trigger on a man before. A cop at that. But I can understand it," Jake said, watching as Kenney notched up his manhood. "You drive to the big city. You break in a big house. Trying to find a parking space probably put too much pressure on you. What happened, Kenney? You get inside and have to piss your pants?"

"Fuck off!" Kenney spit back.

"Brave talk for someone who runs off and leaves his partner. My dog wouldn't even do that," Jake said and watched Kenney lift a rum bottle high above his head.

"Put it down!" Barns shouted. "Kenney!" The shrill, emotion-packed voice echoed through the huge garage. "He'll rip your fuckin' head off. Don't mess with him, Kenney. Not now," Joey said and took away the bottle. He set it on the table. "Why don'tcha go home?" he told Kenney.

Kenney didn't budge, his laser eyes cutting through Jake.

"Go on," Joey urged and pushed him toward the door. "Go on!" Another push. Finally, reluctantly, Kenney left.

Jake waited until he heard the outside door shut, then said, "Kenney doesn't know it, but he owes you a great favor."

"You were gonna shove that bottle down his throat, right?"

"Something like that," Jake said.

Joey nodded. "I figured as much." He rubbed his shoulder, the soreness still there. "Would you really've broken my arm?"

"If I needed to."

"That's what I thought." Joey leaned back against the table, studying the man before him. "Why all the hassle, Eaton?"

"Ex-cons get hassled. Didn't they teach you that in prison?"

"Sure. But the cops've already been here. They come 'round every time somebody runs a stop sign. There's nothin' ta connect me ta Myron Sellers."

"Except an arrest record," Jake reminded him. "From what I hear, Myron ran you in."

"Old news."

"I like to think of it as history. Sometimes history is fascinating. What do you know of history, Joey?"

Joey straightened himself to his full height. "The North won the war," he said.

Jake rolled his shoulders, as if he were about to throw another punch. "Recent history."

Joey's eyes never left Jake. "Such as?"

"Such as why Myron Sellers and you ever worked together. I find that sort of strange, Joey. You're a con and he was sheriff. Doesn't seem a match to me."

Joey stiffened. "Who's bringin' up that old crap?" he demanded.

"It doesn't matter. What matters is the connection. You and Sellers. You and Kenney. Who knows, maybe you and Colin Owens were connected, too."

Joey shook his head. "No way, man. You're not pullin' me inta that."

"Where were you the afternoon Sellers got shot?" Jake asked.

"Here. Workin'."

"Any witnesses?"

"Sure. A hundred," Kenney quipped. "It's standin' room only when I'm under the hood."

"If you want to *stay* standing," Jake told him, "you'd better cut the crap." He let the thought settle, then said, "Start with you and Sellers. How'd you two connect?"

Joey paused, lining up his options. He didn't have any and finally said, "It's like everything else in this rotten hole of a village. It all came down ta money. When ya see a chance ta make a few bucks, ya take it."

Jake thought of Sellers's bank account. "Apparently, Myron was of the same opinion."

"Myron was a crook at heart," Joey spit out. "But I'll give him one thing. He knew like the rest of us that in Winslow, your chances of makin' a few bucks are slim an' none. When one comes along, ya take it."

"Legal or not," Jake speculated.

"Sometimes legal. It didn't matter. But one thing does," Joey said. "I don't want ya pointin' a finger at me 'bout Sellers's murder. If that's the button ya want ta push, I'm callin' my lawyer. You get nothin' more from me."

"I'm listening," Jake said. "Tell me about you and Myron Sellers."

Joey reached for the rum bottle. "Care ta join me?"

"It's a little early," Jake admitted. "But go right ahead."

Joey helped himself while collecting his thoughts. After a second long pull from the bottle, he said, "I ran a few hot loads is all. Workin' for Milly Preston, you prob'ly already heard about it."

Jake looked at Barns with greater interest, thinking back to Sellers's office and the clipping Myron had kept recounting the illegal dumping. "You were involved with that?"

"Not involved." Joey beamed with pride. "I started it. At first it was just ta clean up the place. Until the day he died, my old man never threw nothin' away. I had fifty-gallon drums of antifreeze an' used oil all over the damn place. I had ta do somethin'. I figured, why pay ta have it hauled to a legal landfill? Just load up, drive up in the mountains, an' let it run out on the ground. There's woods up there that've never been walked through. Who's ta care?"

"People like the Prestons," Jake said. "People like Myron Sellers, if he did his job."

Joey sipped more rum. "Oh, Myron did his job all right," he said bitterly. "He caught me. I'd branched out to a few other garages, fixed up an old truck with a false baffle an' a release valve. I could open an' close it without leavin' the cab. I could put down fifteen thousand gallons without gettin' my hands dirty."

"You should be real proud of yourself," Jake said facetiously.

"You don't have ta like it," Joey said. "I was providin' a service an' keepin' my customers happy."

"Who were they?" Jake asked.

Joey shrugged. "Places here an' there. Places just like you're standin' in. Nothin' big."

"You mean nothing on the scale of what an Otis Woodbine could do," Jake said, fishing. "Ever heard of Otis Woodbine, Joey?"

Joey's eyes narrowed. He shook his head unconvincingly. "No. Why would you ask that?"

"Just trying to put some pieces together," Jake answered honestly. "Otis was a hauler, too. Big time. His son, Frazer, has had me followed ever since I came to Winslow. Strange, don't you think?"

Joey stepped back nervously. "I never heard of the guy. The old man, the son. None of 'em."

"How about Colin Owens?" Jake pressed.

"Look." Joey was twisting in the breeze. "I'm tired of answerin' questions, all right?"

"Not 'all right.' Not even close," Jake told him. "It's a lifestyle thing, Joey. That's the only way to look at it. Your style is that of a criminal. Petty. Small time, but a criminal all the same. Myron Sellers and Colin Owens were into something up to their necks. Most likely illegal. That's two more criminals, Joey. Birds of a feather, you know what I mean?"

"I didn't 'know' Owens, all right? I'd seen him around, but I never had any dealin's with him. That's the truth."

"Seen him around where?"

"Winslow. Not often. Once every couple a months or so."

"But you did deal with Myron?"

"Had too. I told ya, Myron caught onta my moonlightin' an' wanted a piece a the action. I went along or he was goin' ta run me in. Turns out," Joey said, "it was one a my better business moves. Myron warmed ta runnin' loads like butter meltin' under the sun. He'd call folks who had places up here an' ask 'em if there was anything he could do or watch out for if they weren't goin' ta make it up ta their property on the weekend. He'd find the no-shows an' off we'd go. He got so good at schedulin' the runs, he suggested we bring in a second driver."

"Let me guess," Jake said. "You brought in Russell Oaks."

"Pretty good," Joey admitted. "You been doin' your homework."

Jake ignored the compliment. "Why Russell?" he wanted to know.

"No reason."

"Had he been in trouble with Sellers, too?"

"Not that I know of."

"And that's something you'd know, isn't it, Joey?"

"Most likely. Yeah, I'd know it."

"Then why bring in Oaks?"

"I wouldn't have, man. That's the damn truth. Myron was callin' all the shots. He wanted Oaks an' he got him. But I wasn't complainin'. We was runnin' day an' night, makin' some serious bucks along the way. Fact is, it only worked as long as it did 'cause Myron could play a real good Andy Taylor of Mayberry findin' out which landowners were goin' ta be away. We'd pick their places an' drive up without a care an' do our business. Simple as that."

"If it was so simple, why didn't it last?" Jake asked.

Joey's expression turned sour. "Russell Oaks got a case a the stupids," he snarled. "All of a sudden, he can't tell left from right an' ends up dumpin' on the wrong property."

"Oliver Preston's?"

"Damn right. Next thing ya know, that old bastard Oliver Preston is on our trail, sniffin' around. Myron was afraid Oliver was goin' ta find out who was behind all the dump sites, so we shut down. Only that wasn't enough for Preston. He wanted hides nailed ta the barn. He wanted somebody ta pay, so he hired a photographer ta take pictures of the sites as evidence."

"Sounds like Oliver was gearing up for a trial."

"He was. He wanted Russell on the stand so everything would come out. Myron an' me was scared shitless. Old man Preston was a bulldog."

"Then why did Oliver agree to a plea?" Jake asked. "If Russell cops out, he never takes the stand."

"All's I know is one day Oliver Preston is wavin' some aerial photographs in Myron's face. They were shoutin' at each other, really goin' at it. A few days later, old man Preston has his tail between his legs acceptin' a plea from Oaks. No trial. No witness stand. No nothin'."

"Until years later, when Colin Owens gets back in an airplane and takes another batch of photos," Jake said. "What would you know about those pictures, Joey?"

"Nothin'."

"How about Russell Oaks? Think he knows anything about some aerial photographs?"

"How would I know?"

Jake shrugged. "I think I should ask him. Where's Russell Oaks now?"

"No idea."

Jake frowned. "Joey, I want to talk to Russell Oaks. I want to talk now."

"Really, man. I'm tellin' the truth. All I know is that he pulled his old pickup in here 'bout a month ago. It was one of those 'when you get to it, work on it' sorta things. Then, after Sellers went down, he came in here an' wanted it right then, so I dropped everything an' got to it. Elizabeth went out for a while an' came back with his clothes in a duffel bag. Russ tossed the bag in the back an' drove off without so much as a word."

"Did he have a gun with him?"

"What difference does it make?"

"The gun Sellers was killed with hasn't been found. Was Oaks armed?" Jake asked again.

"He had a rifle in the window rack."

"Anything else?"

"Not much . . . a few supplies, maybe. The mountains are pretty big, ya know."

"And you figure he might have driven up there and gotten lost for a few days?" Jake asked.

"He might. If that's what his wife said he oughta do, that's what he did."

"Could she have told him to kill Myron Sellers?"

"She could, but why would she?"

"I don't know," Jake answered. "Lottie had reason to hate him, maybe Elizabeth did, too."

"Don't read nothin' in that," Joey said. "Lottie hates everything an' always has. The wonder is that Old John didn't shoot himself sooner justa get away from her," he said as Watson's throaty growl roared into sharp, deep, attacking barks.

Jake drew his .44. "Who are you expecting?"

"Nobody. Honest."

Jake motioned Joey toward the sliding doors. "Open 'em," he said.

"I don't want no trouble. Not here."

Jake shoved Joey forward and stepped in behind him. "Unlock 'em and step to the side."

Joey did as he was told.

In seconds the sliding door cracked open. A man stepped through and opened the door all the way. Jake could see the second man's rifle pointed right at Watson, who was bent low, ready to pounce. Jake recognized the two as the ChemTrol bodyguards.

"Mr. Woodbine don't like being stood up," said the guard inside the door.

Jake had his gun aimed for a chest shot. "Keep talking," he said.

"You don't need the gun."

"That's for me to decide," Jake told him, the revolver still aimed at the man's chest. "I don't like people threatening my partner. Makes me nervous." Silence. "Real nervous," Jake warned.

The man lifted the rifle and stepped back to the Ford. "You get one break, Eaton, and that was it. Follow us," he said. "You'll find it worth your while."

The men waited as Jake went to his Saab and got in. He started the car and pulled in behind them. After shifting into fourth, he gave Watson a pat.

"Frazer Woodbine's a persistent man," Jake told his partner. "Let's see what all the urgency is about."

Watson agreed with a bark.

"Tell me about it," Jake said, sliding the Saab into fifth gear.

—18—

ChemTrol Industries was housed in a modern red brick office park that Frazer Woodbine developed just outside of Nashua, New Hampshire, on Route 101. From Winslow it took two hours. Jake pulled in a visitor's slot and entered the building with Watson at his side. The two bodyguards led the way past a cute receptionist busily watering the potted ferns that lined the spacious lobby.

"Would you look?" Her voice was high and curious. "A puppy dog. People don't usually come in with their puppy dogs. What's his name?" she asked, reaching out to pet him.

"Watson," Jake said.

"Really?" Watson sniffed her ankles. "I think he likes me," she gushed. She patted him and started talking like a baby. Watson gave her a pained look and trotted over to Jake. Watson hated baby talk and babies pulling his ears.

"Maybe he doesn't like me," she said and went back to her watering. The bodyguards waited in front of an office door, then stepped aside so that Jake could enter. The receptionist's office was empty; he imagined that it belonged to the plant lady. The guards closed in behind him and followed him to the far wall. Beige vertical blinds covered the expanse of glass. A security camera mounted near the ceiling captured every move.

Through one partially opened blind, Jake could see Frazer Woodbine. Jake knew it was Frazer without ever having seen him before. It was the way Frazer moved in confident strides, as if he were a general inspecting the troops.

Frazer opened the glass door. "You wait outside," he told the two men. He stepped aside for Jake and Watson to enter. Woodbine closed the door and motioned for Jake to follow. It was an office fit for any CEO—big, with statements of success everywhere. Jake took a seat opposite the polished cherry desk. Watson lay near Jake, his paws stretched out in front of him on the thick blue carpet.

Frazer adjusted his tie and picked a speck from the cuff of his gray suit. He looked like a banker, not a disreputable dumper. He was maybe fifty years old, five foot eleven, 180 pounds, with a powerfully deep voice that bounced out in snappy jerks.

"I prefer to get right to it," Woodbine said, sitting down behind his desk.

"Fine," Jake stated. "Let's start with your bodyguards."

"Security guards," Woodbine corrected. "We deal with quite a lot of sensitive information in this line of work. Most companies don't want it known what they routinely dispose of. Bad public relations, you understand. Security is a high priority." Woodbine pointed to another security camera sweeping the office.

Jake had already taken it in. "So's my life."

"I don't doubt it, but I fail to see the connection."

"The connection is your two goons."

"Really?" Woodbine mused.

Jake sat motionless. "I think they tried to finish me off with a hit-and-run."

Frazer knew better. "You're mistaken," he said calmly. "Mickey and Ron uphold the law. They never stand in the way of it. I'd fire them if they did, and they know it."

Jake had no real evidence, only a hunch, and pushed on. "Then they're working on their own," he suggested. "Doing a little free-lancing."

"They work for me," Woodbine said emphatically.

"Then what were they doing in Winslow?"

"Following my orders."

"Did those orders include tailing me the moment I left Terry Owens's house?"

Woodbine smiled, liking the game. "You don't give up, do you?"

"You'd do well to keep that in mind," Jake cautioned.

"Oh, it's in my mind, Mr. Eaton. In fact, I respect you for it. Tenacity is a trait we share." Woodbine's expression brightened. "There's nothing quite like struggling toward some goal that's always out of reach, then—miraculously—it's in your grasp. Do you find that true?"

Jake did. "Sometimes," he said.

"Then you'll understand why I sent Mickey and Ron to Winslow. Not—as you foolishly imagine—to cause you harm. Far from it. I sent them there to protect my interests."

Jake hazarded a guess. "Real estate interests?"

"Why do you ask?"

Jake told him Mildreth's admission that Woodbine had been an interested buyer in her mountain property. He added what Lieutenant Moreau had speculated. "I heard you already own some land around Winslow," Jake said.

Woodbine shook his head. "Wrong information, Mr. Eaton. True, I have an interest in Mrs. Preston's land, but nothing else in Winslow is worth owning."

"And why is that?"

Woodbine shrugged. "It ought to be obvious. I'm in the waste management business. The Preston name is known worldwide for its concern with environmental causes. Who in my line of work wouldn't want to own—and be associated with—the Oliver Preston legacy?"

"What's held you back?" Jake asked.

Frazer smiled briefly. "The Preston's and I have—what's that overused phrase?—failed to communicate."

Jake remembered Mildreth's bitter expression. "To the point where the Woodbine name is not spoken in Milly's house."

"There you have it," Woodbine admitted, leaning back in his chair. "Difficult to do business under those circumstances."

"And impossible once Mildreth gives the land to the state."

"Which is why I've wanted to speak with you, Mr. Eaton. I want you to intercede on my behalf. I want you to explain to Mrs. Preston that my motives are pure. I'll put up the memorial to her husband, any kind she'd like, plus pay her for the land."

"Generous," Jake said, wondering what Frazer really wanted.

"Not really."

"It might be," Jake cautioned. "It's not just a memorial she wants. She has certain conditions regarding future use of the property. You couldn't develop it. You'd never get your money back."

"Ahh!" Woodbine's eyes brightened with the thought. "That's where you're wrong. Think of it. It's subtle, but goodwill often is."

"Don't you mean PR?" Jake countered. "Associate the name of Oliver Preston with that of Otis Woodbine?"

Frazer stiffened and leaned toward the desk. "Something wrong with that?"

"Depends."

"On?"

"Motive," Jake said flatly. "We're often judged on why we do things, not what we do."

Frazer hesitated, collecting his thoughts. Finally, he spoke solemnly. "All right, Mr. Eaton. Why would I make such an offer to Milly Preston? Answer: pollution. The worst kind—pollution of the mind. Men start rumors that take on a reality all their own. I want to do something that will change the perception that my father was—and by association that I and my company, ChemTrol, are—vile."

"The Woodbine name rings some nasty bells," Jake reminded him.

"My father made some mistakes. No question. But I corrected each one when I founded this company. If I discovered—by some oversight—that we weren't upholding the letter of the law in handling every drop of waste, I made the necessary changes. The *letter of the law,* I stress. We're legal now. Every step. We are also worldwide. ChemTrol operates in all fifty states and in most foreign countries. I can assure you that wouldn't have happened if we weren't playing by the rules. In this business, reputation is everything, and ours is at the top."

"*If* that's true, you have nothing to worry about."

"You doubt me?" Frazer asked. "With what reason?"

"Let's start with the obvious," Jake answered, gesturing to

where Mickey and Ron stood on the other side of the door. "Your two goons outside of Colin Owens's house."

Frazer's eyes narrowed. "So?"

"So they didn't follow me there. They had the house staked out. Question is, were they looking for Colin, too, or anyone else who showed up?"

"Are you asking me if I know Colin Owens?"

"That was next," Jake said.

"No, I do not." Frazer's voice was firm, steady.

"How about Myron Sellers?"

Frazer broke into an uneasy smile. "You're fishing. Wrong bait. Wrong ocean. My interest in Winslow is Preston Mountain, nothing else."

"Then you didn't know Sellers?"

"What difference would it make?"

"Four hundred thousand dollars in a secret Boston account." Jake let the idea simmer. "A man who can afford to buy a mountain could afford that," Jake said, watching Woodbine's uneasy smile soften. "He might," Jake continued, "be very generous if someone—what was your term?—'interceded' on his behalf."

"I'm willing to pay you," Woodbine said.

"It wasn't me I was thinking about. Milly told me that Myron Sellers recommended she sell. You were the buyer. How much did it cost you to put that bug in Sellers's ear?"

The smile disappeared from Woodbine's face. "All right, I knew the sheriff."

"And Colin? And about a certain Boston bank account?"

"You're wasting your time, Mr. Eaton. What you need to know, I've told you. You'll get nothing else."

"Seems a fair trade," Jake said, standing. "That's exactly what you'll get from me. Nothing."

Watson pushed himself up on all fours and followed Jake to the door.

"Shouldn't you let Mrs. Preston decide?"

"I should do a lot of things. Some of them, I don't."

"In this case," Woodbine warned, "you'll be making a mistake."

Jake stepped back to the center of the room. "And you've made several," Jake told him. "I don't like being followed. I like even less being ordered at gunpoint to have this little chat. I don't know what your game is, Woodbine, but once I find out, I'll let Mrs. Preston know."

Frazer, cool as before, didn't react. "Good day, Mr. Eaton."

The hell it is, Jake went out thinking.

—19—

Jake's mood matched the weather: gray, gloomy, with cool rain falling straight down from the windless afternoon sky. As he walked toward Boston Harbor, he felt a peculiar coldness. Even Watson seemed to sag as he padded along the dock, his shiny black coat drawing in the water like a sponge.

Jake jumped a puddle, reached for his marina keys, and stopped at the locked metal gate. In the water below sat *Gamecock*, pulling gently against her mooring lines. Watson stepped toward the gate expectantly, like all the other times, waiting for it to swing open. But Jake hung back, the key in his hand, inches from the lock.

It may have been the rain soaking his clothes, but he felt weary, toyed with. Images of Frazer Woodbine sitting confidently behind his desk hung in Jake's memory. Could it be that all Frazer really wanted was Milly's land? Could it be that Mickey and Ron hadn't been involved in the failed hit-and-run? Could Jake be wrong about his suspicions?

Jake stood thinking, the key no nearer the gate's lock. Absently, he put the key back into his pocket and turned away, stopping only at Watson's throaty bark.

"What's that all about?" Jake asked as the dog raked his right paw against the locked gate. "You want to go in? Go in."

Watson shook the rain from his wet fur. He rolled his head in a slow, circling spiral toward the blue boat, then barked sharply again. Jake stepped forward and put the key in the lock.

"I'll tell you something, pup," Jake told his partner. "Wet dogs and men in bad moods are seldom welcomed with open arms. My advice is to stay the hell away from here."

"Oh? Want my advice?" Gloria was crossing the parking lot. She walked lightly toward Jake, splashing in every puddle like a child.

Watson sped up to her, his tail cranking with joy, his head bobbing submissively. Gloria bent down and grabbed the wet dog in a bear hug. When she let him go, she scooped up a handful of puddled water and splashed it on her front, a smile beaming from her face.

"There," she said to Jake. "That ought to make us about even. I'm wet, and you're soaked." She laughed, splashing herself once again.

Jake looked at her curiously, as if a gargoyle were sprouting from her forehead.

Gloria felt embarrassed for him. Smiling tenderly, she said, "It's all right, Jake. I haven't lost my mind. As a matter of fact, I think I've found it. Part of it, at least."

She stepped to him and put her arms around his neck, draping herself against him. "I can't explain it, really. You'd understand it if you'd been through it; if you haven't, words can't come close to explaining what I've felt like these past few months."

He put his arms around her waist. "Try me," he said.

"All right. It's like I've been in a fog, only it wasn't really. In a fog you get some sensation, but what I felt like had no sensation at all. It was nothing, sprinkled here and there with the clear understanding that there was no hope for me. Hope was irrelevant. My life was one no-exit misery."

Jake held her tighter, clinging to every painful word, trying to understand where the strength of her voice came from.

"You don't just wake up from a nightmare like that," he said.

"No, you don't. Especially when it's not a dream. I was living it, Jake. Maybe living isn't the right word. But that's what I wanted to be doing. I wanted to be alive again." She leaned her head back and looked him in the eye. "You said earlier it's not the size of the step you take, but the direction. That's what I decided to do, take a step."

"And you're still on your feet," he said, encouraging her.

"Barely." As quickly as the joy sang in her voice, it was gone. "I changed my mind a thousand times. Should I? Shouldn't I? Maybe I ought to just stay in bed."

"Why didn't you?"

"Because I care about Milly and my father." She put her head against Jake's shoulder. "Because I care about you. I finally realized that."

Jake rubbed his hands along the small of her back as the rain pelted them hard. He brushed back her wet hair and kissed the softness behind her ear.

Gloria didn't move away, but she said, "Not now."

Jake kissed her on the mouth.

"We have an appointment," she said, after returning the kiss.

Jake was half listening. "With whom?"

"Morrison."

"Who?"

"Professor Morrison." This time, she kissed Jake, then stepped back from him. "It's important," she said.

"So are you." He was staring into her eyes. "You make me very happy."

Her own sense of happiness spread across her face. "You're not listening," she said.

"I am."

"This is serious."

"So, tell me." He tried for one more kiss, but Gloria held him back, her arms straight against his chest. The rain poured down her cheeks and into the corners of her mouth. "You're all wet," Jake told her.

She ignored him. "Professor Morrison is a geologist."

"Okay." His voice was soft.

"I was getting into my car to go to Cambridge to see you when I heard Watson at the gate. If you weren't home, I was going to drive the professor to New Hampshire to meet you."

Gloria hauling a professor to New Hampshire got Jake's attention. "What's this all about?" he asked seriously.

"That's what I've been trying to tell you. When I met with my father, he mentioned Professor Morrison as one of Oliver Preston's colleagues at Harvard."

"So?" Jake was hunting for the significance.

"So, I phoned him."

"Why do I want to talk to a geologist?" Jake asked, wiping the rain from his forehead.

"I'll let him explain."

Gloria opened the gate with her key. She took Jake by the hand and led him down the ramp as Watson flew past them. Watson loved running across the floating docks.

"Where are we going?" Jake asked, following her.

"To get some dry clothes. You left a couple of things on board."

Jake walked beside her. "Gloria?"

"Don't say it, Jake. Whatever it is, don't say it. Not yet. It's one step and one day. Let's just leave it at that for now. Okay?"

"I just wanted to say I'm proud of you."

Gloria hesitated, then kissed him warmly. Jake responded, his tongue gliding along the inside of her lips, until some magnetic surge pulled them closer together. They held each other tightly as the dock rose and fell gently on the slow movement of a wake.

Jake kissed her harder now, held her against him, felt her press herself on him with a rise and fall all her own.

"Come on," Jake said, leading her toward the boat. "The geologist can wait."

— 20 —

The cab stopped on Bow Street a few blocks from Harvard Square. Jake paid the fare, got out, and held the door for Gloria. Towel dried and well fed, Watson stayed onboard *Gamecock*. No wine with dinner this time, which suited him fine.

Gloria took Jake's arm and hurried him into a cavernous basement office filled with stacks of bound reports, books, and one Professor Warren W. Morrison. The professor was a round man in his early sixties. He had a black-gray beard, a kind face framed by rimless glasses, and narrow-set inquisitive eyes that darted across his computer screen when Jake and Gloria entered.

Without getting up, the professor greeted them both with a weak handshake. But they hadn't made the trip seeking signs of virility; they'd come because Gloria needed to. This was her show, her small step. She had told Jake about the professor during the cab ride over.

According to Gloria, Morrison earned his Ph.D. in geology from the Massachusetts Institute of Technology and now taught at Harvard. Through his connection with the Wilderness Association for Environmental Sanity—an organization that Oliver Preston founded—Professor Morrison had become an expert on the geological composition of disposal sites. More importantly, he had been Oliver Preston's oldest and closest friend.

Gloria thanked Morrison for seeing them, then said, "Tell Jake what you told me, professor."

"Please do," Jake stated, still wondering what he was doing in a geologist's office.

Gloria caught Jake's disgruntled tone. "Tell him about the models, professor. The ones you and Oliver worked out."

"Yes, yes, of course." Morrison pecked at the computer keys, his attention on the color monitor as a series of numerical equations raced across it. In seconds, the screen changed from numbers to a recognizable design.

"What you're looking at," Professor Morrison began, "is a computer model of what the Environmental Protection Agency considers a safe disposal site. As you can see, it's a lined rectangular pit. The lining's impervious. Whatever goes into the pit stays in. When it's full, it gets covered over, sodded, and, in some places, turned into golf courses. In the best case scenario, you never know it's there."

"I'm not dealing with golf courses," Jake noted bluntly. "I'm dealing with murder."

Morrison's eyes glistened as he gazed at Jake with a hard grin. "I don't think you know what you're dealing with, Mr. Eaton. Murder might be the least of it."

Jake and Gloria exchanged a quick glance. His indifference to this Cambridge trip had turned to admiration, and Gloria knew it.

"Please," Jake said, "go on."

"Thank you." Morrison turned back to his computer. "I've shown you the best-case scenario of handling a waste site, but that is not what Oliver and I spent most of our research time on. We were interested in worst cases—dumping toxics where there is no lining, for example."

"Like up on Preston Mountain," Jake added.

"Correct." Morrison's fingers plucked away. On the screen appeared a dark rectangle with leaks pouring out like murky streams. Morrison tapped the screen with a slender finger. "See there how waste moves? Poison in, poison out."

"Frightening," said Gloria, her eyes locked on the screen.

"Quite," Morrison agreed. "And all very unscientific. Take, for example, the number of legal landfills in the United States alone. The EPA estimates eighty thousand, but that's not counting the illegal ones. Oliver's research estimated there to be over one hundred thousand. Maybe as high as one hundred fifty thousand legal and illegal sites combined."

Jake watched the monitor at the picture of a tanker truck passing the landfill. A spigot opened and dark electronic drops sprayed out the back of the truck.

"Moonlighters," Jake said.

"That they are," Morrison affirmed. "Used to be part of growing up in the South. Waste oil was sprayed on unpaved roads to keep down the dust. Now they're everywhere, as Oliver found out. Have truck, will travel—pick up a few bucks along the way. Even if the dump sites are up on Preston Mountain," the professor said sourly.

"But those were stopped," Jake reminded him.

Morrison said querulously, "So most believed. Oliver, for example, had his doubts that the dumping on his land, and on land around his, ever stopped."

"How could that be?" Gloria asked, shrinking a little into herself, some of her earlier spark fading.

"Exactly," Jake chimed in. "Not hours ago, I spoke to one of the drivers. Out of concern that Oliver might have hunted them all down, he swears the dumping stopped."

"Maybe it did . . . in one form." The professor dragged the mouse to an icon and clicked. A cargo ship appeared, complete with small, uniform waves lapping at its hull. Morrison clicked again and fifty-five-gallon drums rolled from the stern and sank to the bottom. "Terrible stuff," he said. "Medical syringes ending up on the beaches is a fraction of it. Outer space is a junkyard; the ocean is a dumping ground. If we are God's experiment, he must be hellishly disappointed."

"But why?" Gloria asked. "Why do people do it?"

"Money," Morrison answered flatly. "Hiding poison is a fifteen-billion-dollar-a-year business. Money like that draws all kinds. And some of them are very, very clever. Here." The professor's attention was back on the screen. "Look at what's coming up," he said, punching in a new set of numbers. Soon a graphic appeared of a syringe dropping from the sky sticking into the ground. "What you see on the monitor is a simplified version of deep well injections. Either of you ever heard of them?"

"Never," Jake admitted. Gloria shook her head, uncomfortable with the grim knowledge that she felt was coming.

"It's simple really, and horrifying if improperly used," Morrison said as the plunger of the syringe pushed the liquid through the needle and deep into the earth.

"Looks like the reverse of drilling a well."

"Precisely, Mr. Eaton. Instead of drilling a hole to remove something, we drill a hole to put something in under extremely high pressure. Thousands of pounds per square inch. Liquid waste is literally driven into porous rock such as lime or soapstone."

"The idea is disgusting," Gloria said.

The professor looked up at her and stated solemnly, "It's the deadliest assault ever undertaken on the earth's environment."

"Why doesn't someone stop it?" Jake asked.

"Because it fits right in with human nature," Morrison answered. "When we don't like something, or don't know exactly how to deal with it, we dispose of it."

"Out of sight, out of mind," Jake offered.

Morrison nodded. "Correct. The second reason is it's a relatively easy technology to apply. The Defense Department has experimented with injection wells nearly three miles deep. What they put in them was top secret, but you can bet it wasn't Perrier."

"Good God." Gloria's voice was a whisper.

"Good God, indeed."

"You said 'if improperly used' they were dangerous. What's the proper method?" Jake asked.

"Honestly, I'm not sure there is one. What's reasonable about shooting anything toxic miles inside the earth? But if you assume that's the proper thing to do, you look at the geology and find mineral deposits that will act like a sponge. You bring the waste to the site in tanker trucks and start pumping. The soft stone absorbs the toxics; you cap the well, cover it, and go on your way to the next site. If you covered your tracks well enough," Morrison added, "no one would ever know you'd been there."

Jake's expression startled Gloria. "What's the matter, Jake? What is it?"

"I don't know," he said, collecting his thoughts. "Someone with a camera taking aerial photographs might know you'd been there."

For the first time, the professor wasn't following. Jake explained about the two sets of aerial photographs and the Colin Owens break-in of Mildreth's home.

Morrison pushed himself up from his work station, struggling with some vague memory. "Owens? Owens?"

Jake and Gloria looked on as Morrison disappeared behind a hastily piled stack of books and papers. They heard a cabinet door open, papers being shuffled, and Morrison mumbling to himself. Finally, the professor reappeared, his expression thoughtful.

"The name 'Colin Owens,'" he said, shaking his head. "I could've sworn Oliver talked about that man. I thought there might be something on him in the file where Oliver kept his photographs, but all of that must have gone back to his house."

Jake's ears perked up. "You saw the pictures?"

"Years ago. Yes."

"And talked with Oliver about Colin Owens?"

"That's correct."

"What about?"

Morrison ducked his head almost bashfully. "To be honest, I can't remember. It was *so* long ago. The name did ring a bell. The only thing I'm certain of is that Oliver was quite concerned that someone was using his land for experimentation."

"What kind?" Jake asked.

"The very kind I've been talking to you about," Morrison answered. "Deep well injection. Only not into the usual soft, absorbant stone, but into hard, impervious granite."

Gloria's voice cranked up an octave. "That doesn't make sense!" she snapped.

"Does fouling the earth in any way make any sense at all?" Morrison shot back. "Of course not. The method doesn't really matter in such madness as long as it works well enough for the dumper. "Let me show you," the professor continued, back at his computer. He keyed an icon and waited for the screen to fill. In seconds, the cross section of a mountain appeared. "Oliver calculated this model," he said, pointing to various cracks and breaks within the rocks. "These cracks," he said, tracing one with his finger, "are known as fissures. They're like veins of coal running inside a mountain. Large fissures are big enough to hold single-story houses, and they run for miles. The only difference between a coal filled vein and a fissure is that a fissure is empty."

The image hit Jake hard. "You could pour thousands of gallons into a space like that," he said.

"Not thousands, *billions*. The Russians have such a site in Mayak in the Ural Mountains. Conservative estimates are that it's injected with over eight billion gallons of radioactive poisons. *Eight billion gallons*," Morrison repeated. "If it ever seeps into the water supply, the human tragedy would be uncalculable."

Gloria stepped back and turned away. Jake dug in. "Oliver *told* you he had such suspicions?" Jake asked.

"He did."

"Why didn't Mildreth ever mention it?" he wanted to know.

"I don't believe that Oliver ever mentioned it to her," Morrison explained. "The surface dumping was difficult enough for Milly to handle. Oliver said that if, and when, he ever discovered the injection well into a fissure, he'd tell her. But he never found it."

Gloria turned back. "Maybe it isn't there."

Morrison nodded. "Perhaps. All I know is that Oliver had his reasons to think otherwise."

"Did he ever tell you what those reasons were?" Jake asked.

"Tracks from heavy machinery. Matted-down grass where they'd been. It all showed up in the photographs he'd had taken for the trial."

Jake glanced at Gloria, an idea forming in his mind. "One of the drivers—Joey Barns—told me that Oliver confronted Sellers with some photographs. Immediately afterward, Oliver decided against going to trial."

"So?" Gloria asked.

"So it doesn't add up. You press your case when you've got the evidence. Those pictures provided all the evidence Oliver needed that illegal dumping had taken place. So what does he do?" Jake said. "He does the opposite and lets everybody walk with a slap on the wrist."

"It was a decision that Oliver regretted," Morrison said. "It bothered him until the day he died."

"Then why did he do it?" Jake wondered.

Morrison shook his head. "I don't have an answer."

"I'd settle for an educated guess," Jake said. "Care to offer one?"

"I deal in facts, Mr. Eaton," Morrison said. "The only fact I'm certain of is that if there is an injection well up on Preston Mountain, and if it's tapped into a giant fissure, it could seep poison for miles, endangering the health of thousands throughout New England."

"It's all so horrible," Gloria fretted.

"Which is why I said that one murder may be the least of your worries." Morrison was looking at Jake. "You've got to do what Oliver never could. You've got to find out if there's an injection well on that land."

The cab driver taking Jake and Gloria back to *Gamecock* made another wrong turn, this time heading south down Atlantic Avenue. The foreign-born cabbie pulled over and stopped in front of Rowes Wharf. Disgustedly he slammed his fist on the dash and shut off the meter, signaling that his battle with being lost in Boston traffic was over.

Jake paid the man, tipped him generously out of sympathy, not for service, and got out. Gloria was waiting on the curb. The meeting with Professor Morrison had left her gaunt and tired.

Jake closed the car door, and the cab sped off. He and Gloria walked the few remaining blocks toward the marina. They strode along silently until Gloria finally spoke.

"That was nice of you," she said.

Jake was distracted. "What was nice?"

"A ten-dollar tip."

"Is that what I gave him?" He acted genuinely surprised. "I wasn't paying attention."

"You always pay attention," she corrected. "Why so generous?"

Jake, digging his hands deep into his pants pockets, looked down solemnly at Gloria. "I know what it feels like to be lost," he said, thinking of all Professor Morrison had told him. "I didn't mention this before, but I had a meeting with Frazer Woodbine just before I came to see you."

"*The* Frazer Woodbine?" she queried.

Jake looked at her curiously. "You know him?"

"Not well."

"I suppose you're like Milly and don't mention the Woodbine name in your house either."

"Now, why would I do that?"

"Because of the nasty business he's in," Jake told her.

"Real estate isn't all that nasty," she teased.

Jake stopped. "Real estate?"

"That's right. Frazer was a big player a few years back. He bargain hunts all over the country, buying land mostly."

"Interesting," Jake mused.

"Not really," Gloria added. "My father does the same thing. Land is the only thing you can't make more of. When a good deal comes along, you take it."

"Woodbine would buy Preston Mountain even if it was a bad deal," Jake said, looking out into the harbor at the tugs working their way along.

Gloria leaned against the retaining wall, nudging a pebble into the water below. It sent out small concentric ripples.

"What are you thinking?" Jake asked.

"I don't know." She shrugged slightly.

"Yes, you do."

Finally, she said, "I was just wondering how Milly would take it if what Professor Morrison said was even half true."

Jake had the same worry. "What if her vision for Oliver's memory, his memorial, were to be built on a toxic time bomb?"

Gloria couldn't shake the thought. It had settled in her mind like a snag in silk and wouldn't go away. "If millions of gallons are—"

"Try billions."

"I can't even imagine it," she said, looking up at Jake. "What was it Morrison said?"

"Injection wells are the deadliest assault ever undertaken on the earth's environment."

"You've got to do something, Jake."

"I'm going to, right after I get you home and tuck you in."

"You're not staying?"

"Not tonight. Like you said, I've got to do something, and I know what it is. Come on, I'll take you home and pick up Watson. He's about to earn his keep."

—21—

It was just after midnight when Jake drove past the ChemTrol office park. He made sure that no lights were on, then turned around at the first opportunity and drove back to the parking lot. He switched off his headlights, circled the lot, and found it empty except for the tan Ford. He drove to the far end, parked next to a retaining wall, and got out. Watson jumped down and stood at close heel.

The night air was chilly. Jake eased the car door closed, listened for sounds, and watched for movement from the shadows. Nothing.

"So far, so good," he said to Watson and motioned him forward along the base of the retaining wall. The dog's black coat in the shadows would be impossible to make out. Watson crept along without a sound.

Quickly, Jake moved into the open, ignoring his partner's silent progress. The metal side door was fifty feet ahead and well hidden behind dense landscaping. Jake edged along the mountain laurel, then jogged the last few feet in partial view of the camera mounted on the building's side. He ducked out of sight behind a stand of shrubs and waited. In seconds, Watson pulled up beside him, hidden by darkness and Jake's purposeful blundering. Jake knew if he broke in, every alarm in the ChemTrol fortress would ring out. The only solution was to be let in.

Jake directed the dog with a hand signal to a spot next to the door. He pulled out the steel pick from his pocket and worked on the lock. He stopped, listened, and worked on it again, making slightly more noise. This time, he got what he wanted: an opened door with Mickey the security guard standing on the other side. In that same instant, Watson was in the air.

"Jesus!" the guard hollered in complete surprise as both dog and Jake's Magnum slammed into him, knocking him dazed to the floor. Jake stepped inside and closed the door. Watson stood over Mickey, his snout curled back in a snarl. Jake stepped on the guard's wrist, lifted the gun from his hand, and tucked it in his own waistband.

"Thank you," Jake baited, waving Watson off. "The control room for security," he said, serious now. "Where is it?"

Mickey glared back at Jake's .44. He had no choice but to answer. "That way." He motioned with his head.

"Lead on."

Mickey crawled to his feet, his eyes flicking from Jake to the black dog.

"How many guards are there?" Jake asked as they moved cautiously down the hall.

"Just me and my partner. Equipment does all the hard work."

"Where is your partner?"

"Doing rounds."

"Coming back when?" Silence. Jake didn't like the hesitation. "Careful now. We don't want anyone getting hurt, but it'll be you if it comes to that. When's your buddy coming back?"

"Fifteen minutes," he said, stopping at the door to security control. He opened it. Jake and Watson followed him into a room filled with wall monitors providing pictures from at least fifteen different camera locations.

Jake scanned the black and white images. "If he's out there doing rounds, how come I don't see him?"

"Monitor eighteen."

Jake took a closer look. Guard number two sat leaning back, feet up on a pulled-out desk drawer, reading a girlie magazine. "All right," Jake said. "Let's get moving."

"Where to?"

"Woodbine's office. I thought it strange that he had a security camera in his own private office. Makes a man wonder what's all that important." Jake waved the barrel of his .44 in Mickey's direction. "Turn off the camera. I don't want any record of me being inside."

"I'll know you're inside," Mickey spit back.

"You don't count," Jake teased. "You, my boy, let me in. Now, shut down the system."

Mickey stepped to the bank of toggle switches and snapped off a cluster. The monitors showing Woodbine's office went dim, then blank. The tape decks stopped recording.

Jake looked at his watch. "All right," he said. "Your partner's due back in fifteen, we'll be gone in ten. Let's go."

They moved silently down the hall toward the receptionist's office. At it, the reluctant guard opened the door with his key. "You won't get away with this," he warned.

"We'll see." Jake pushed him inside and closed the door. He moved quickly to Frazer's private office. "I haven't got all day," Jake cautioned as Mickey unlocked the door. Jake pointed to a chair. "Have a seat." Mickey slouched in the chair. "Watson."

The dog's head snapped up.

"Watch him."

Mickey eyed the obedient dog with disdain as Watson positioned himself in front of the chair, his sharp eyes locked on the guard. Jake sat at Frazer's desk. He put down the Magnum within easy reach in front of him and opened the top drawer.

"What are you looking for?" Mickey wanted to know.

"Connections," Jake said. "Preston Mountain. Winslow. Woodbine. It all has a nice ring to it, don't you think?"

"I think you're crazy."

"Could be. Could be I'm right on target." Jake flipped through the few miscellaneous papers and closed the top drawer, then he opened the ones on the side. "I recently had a *very* interesting conversation with a Harvard professor. You know Harvard, don't you, Mickey? A lot of old brick buildings on the Cambridge side of the Charles River. You ought to swing by some time. Might do you good."

"Fuck off."

"It did me wonders. Yes, it did. It got me thinking in an entirely different way about one thing and another. Take Frazer, for example. He's a troubled man. Things are going along so well for him, and then all hell breaks loose. Why?" Jake dug around in one of the drawers as he continued talking. "At first I thought it was because Mildreth Gibbon Preston wouldn't sell him her property." He looked up at Mickey. "Your boss even went so far as to have Myron Sellers put in a good word for him. He asked me, too. I won't, of course, but it did start me asking a different kind of question."

"What the hell is that?" Mickey spit out.

"The question is, what happened that makes Frazer want that mountain so damn bad? It's not the memorial to Oliver. Frazer said he'd put one up himself."

"Must be something else."

"Very good," Jake mocked. "Harvard may give you a scholarship." He closed another drawer. "The answer is the state. Milly's giving the land away to New Hampshire. What do you think will happen if the state ends up owning that land and finds they just got title to twenty thousand poisoned acres?"

Mickey scrunched his shoulders and said gruffly, "I don't know what the hell you're talking about."

Jake ignored him. "You'll be on the hot seat, Mick. You—your boss, you name it. The state will come down on you with everything they've got. If I were you . . ." Jake stopped, his attention drawn to a piece of paper in the drawer. It was a regular-sized white sheet, but what demanded attention was its crumpled appearance. It had obviously been wadded, smoothed out, and saved. Curious, Jake thought and picked it up. It read in simple handwriting, "Fire tower at noon. Bring the money, or you'll never get back what you want."

Before Jake put down the note, he heard a voice other than Mickey's ask, "Find what you want?" It was the second guard, Ron, aiming a 9mm automatic at Jake's forehead. He seemed to be enjoying every second. "Get to your feet," Ron commanded. "Very slowly."

The hair inched up on Watson's neck as a mean growl rumbled

deep inside him. Mickey pushed himself further back into his chair as Jake spoke. "Two against two seems fair," Jake said, putting the rumpled note over the .44.

"No dice," Ron said. "Push that cannon across the desk, then get up. Another stunt like that, and—"

Jake was getting to his feet when Mickey blurted out, "Watch him, Ronnie, he's got my—"

Jake dropped to the floor, dragging Mickey's revolver from his waistband. Above him, shots from Ron's automatic split the room, tearing wood, missing their mark. Judging from Mickey's whimper and Watson's ferocious snarls and barks, the dog might be the next target.

Jake wasted no time, his senses sharp as surgical instruments. In an instant, he slid left to the side of the desk. In a movement so fluid and swift it was a blur, Jake raised the revolver and fired once. The bullet caught Ron in the left shoulder and hurled him against the wall amidst shouts of pain. Jake slithered to his feet and kicked the 9mm out of the guard's reach. One perfect motion later, he swung his leg up and connected with Mickey, who was struggling to leave his chair. Mickey grabbed his throat where the blow had struck, gasping for air.

Jake raced back for the Magnum, picked it up, and shouted to Watson. "Let's go!" He tossed Mickey's gun down the hall, then took off in the opposite direction, threw open the side door, and ran quickly to his Saab. When Watson jumped across the front seat, Jake piled in behind him and fired up the engine. He drove a hundred yards down the highway before switching on the headlights and shifting smoothly into fifth.

Jake was halfway to Winslow before his heart slowed, but his thoughts were clearer than ever. No matter how he approached it, no matter which angle he took, he could think of only one man who would have sent that note to Frazer Woodbine, and it was Russell Oaks, the man off hiding in the mountains. Jake only hoped that he wasn't too late to stop him as he sped toward the village.

He rolled through Winslow doing eighty and skidded to a stop in front of the Oaks's house. He shut off the engine and got out,

Watson at his side. The silence was intense, the quarter moon bright and shiny, the air cold.

At the front door, he saw blue TV lights dance against a wall. He didn't knock and he didn't hesitate. He went in, splintering the doorjamb on his way. Watson instinctively darted toward the light.

The TV was in the kitchen. Elizabeth half turned when Jake and the black dog came toward her. She leaped for the kitchen knife when she saw who it was. Jake's hand hit the knife at the same instant hers did. For a small woman, her strength was impressive, but she was no match as he pried open her fingers and disarmed her.

She looked at Jake, her eyes popping. "Get out!" She pulled the floor-length robe tight around her.

"Not tonight, kiddo. Too much has changed, and you're right in the middle of it. Where's your husband?"

"I don't know."

"Has he been here?"

"No."

"Are you lying to me?"

"No. And I don't know what you're talking about!" She was clipping her angry words.

"I think you do," Jake said. "Blackmail's not all that hard to understand." Elizabeth turned away from Jake's searching eyes. "I want what you have, Mrs. Oaks. Whatever it is, I want it. Give it to me, then I'll deal with Woodbine my way."

She looked back at Jake. "Get out of my house," she said, her voice steady.

"Not until we have a little talk." Jake put his hands on her shoulders and forced her into a chair. He straddled another and sat across from her at the kitchen table. Watson paced the room.

"I broke into ChemTrol's office tonight," Jake said, taking the crumpled paper from his shirt pocket and showing it to her. "Money, Mrs. Oaks. You think it's your turn to go to the bank. Well, let me tell you something. Frazer Woodbine's not going to let you walk away with one cent. Not if what you have could ruin him."

She glared at Jake as if trying to see him through dense fog. "What makes you think Russell and I have anything to do with this?"

"The fire tower for one thing. Who's idea was that? Russell's? He's up in the mountains already, staking it out, making himself a plan. What'd he think? It's so isolated that he'd somehow have the advantage over Woodbine and his men? Turn that around, Mrs. Oaks. Say everything goes wrong. Say Russell doesn't come out. Twenty thousand acres is a lot of land in which to hide a body."

Elizabeth's eyes widened. "Nobody's going to get hurt!" she snapped. "We made that clear."

Jake leaned back, satisfied with his hunch. "Then you are involved."

"As if you didn't already know. You probably work for Woodbine, too."

"If I did, I wouldn't have put a bullet in one of his guards tonight," Jake said, watching the slightest doubt grow in Elizabeth's expression. "You don't believe me, do you?"

"I don't know what to believe or who to believe." She started to get up and Jake grabbed her arm. "I need to check on my children," she shot back at him.

Jake didn't let go. "Where are they?" he asked.

"In the bedroom."

"Go ahead."

She got up, stepped quietly to the door, looked in, and came back, moving more calmly now, more assured. "They're Russell's pride and joy," she said. "We want the money for them. We want to be able to get them out of here."

"Blackmail's not a very good start."

"Being born in Winslow is worse."

Jake let the thought hang. "What have you got that Woodbine's willing to pay for?"

She leaned against the counter. "Some papers."

"What kind of papers?"

"I don't know. That's the truth. Numbers is all I know."

"Where'd you get the papers?" Jake asked.

Elizabeth lifted her hands in submission. "Wait. You're going too fast for me. I've got to think."

"There may not be time," Jake told her.

"Why not?"

"When's the exchange supposed to be?"

"Today at noon."

Jake checked his watch. "That gives us only a few hours to come up with a new scheme."

"We? I didn't say you could get involved with any of this. No way."

"I am involved whether you like it or not. But more importantly, you've got to start trusting somebody. I may be the only option you have, and I'm not a patient man. What's it going to be, Mrs. Oaks?"

"It's going to be your ass," she said thoughtfully.

Joey Barns stepped out from behind the bedroom door, pointing a shotgun at Jake's chest. "And I'm going to hand it to you," Joey said, smiling.

Jake didn't hesitate as Joey jacked a shell into the breech. Jake upended the kitchen table and dove swiftly to the left as the shotgun blast tore into the table, sending Watson scampering for cover.

As Joey pumped another shell, Jake pivoted into him with a spin kick designed to stop at his backbone. The wind gushed out of Barns and he slammed hard against the wall, sending the shotgun skittering into the hall, where Kenney Ruggles picked it up.

Jake was off balance when he lunged and caught a swiftly rising foot. A trace of blood settled in the corner of his mouth and an echo rang in his ear, still he managed to stagger Kenney with a right hook. Kenney swung the gun butt, but Jake blocked it and rushed forward. Kenney head-faked, but Jake nailed him again and went for the shotgun as Kenney stumbled against the counter. Jake had the barrel in his hands when Elizabeth chopped down with a crockery bowl.

Jake dropped to the ground in a world gray and blurry. He wasn't out, but with the shotgun unaccounted for, he didn't move. Jake hoped Watson wouldn't either.

"What now?" Kenney's voice was all nerves.

"Shut up, Ken."

"No, you answer. What the hell now?"

Elizabeth was plainly weary. "Shut up! Shut up, both of you. I've got to think."

"Lot of good thinkin' did," Kenney spit out. "You said it'd be Woodbine's men comin' around, huntin' for those papers."

"I know what I said." She glared at him. "I also told you to shut up."

"You said ta be ready for Woodbine's men, but this fucker's a cop."

"I know who he is, Joey."

"Yesterday in my garage, he damn near tore my arm off. What the hell are we gonna do with him now?" Joey persisted.

Elizabeth tossed off her robe, trying to answer that very question as she did so. She was completely dressed under it except for socks and shoes, which she wrestled into now, standing on one foot at a time and balancing. It was the chance Jake had waited for. They wouldn't shoot at him if she was too close, and she was right next to him. He rolled into her and sent her crashing to the floor. The sudden change caught all of them off guard and left Jake standing over her with the shotgun in his hands aimed at Joey and Kenney. Watson stood over Elizabeth, his teeth showing through a whispery snarl.

"Playtime's over, all right?" Nobody blinked. Nobody moved. "When I was first in this business, my wife and I got jumped by three toughies just like you. Each one had a knife. Each one had some fun waving it in my wife's face. I didn't think it was fun at all and said so. They didn't expect a gun. When I pulled it, one of them grabbed her and slipped a blade under her throat. And there we were, jockeying with the fear that was between us. Who'd give? Who'd do something stupid? Who'd back off that first step? It's that step that kills—not the gun, not the knife. It's that step away from fright that gives away the edge." Jake glared at each of them. "I don't want to hurt any of you. I don't even like the thought of it. But I will, and I want that understood."

Joey pulled in a short breath. "What happened ta the three guys?"

"Same thing that will happen if you move. I pulled the trigger."

Jake called off Watson and told Elizabeth to stand. "Take your belts off." Kenney and Joey did as told. "Tie their hands," he ordered Elizabeth. She took their belts and tied them as tight as she could.

When she was finished, Jake checked the knots, then lead Joey and Kenney to the bedroom. "This is the children's room. I don't want to hear a peep." He shoved them in and closed the door.

Back in the kitchen, he set up the table and ejected the shells from the shotgun. He laid the empty gun on the counter and lowered himself into a chair.

"Sit down," he snapped. Elizabeth did. "Now, what the hell's going on here?" Jake asked and waited for answers.

—22—

Elizabeth sat with her eyes closed. When she opened them, the whites were wide around her greenish gray irises. She'd bitten her lower lip, bitten back the bitterness and anger. There was no pretense now, no room to maneuver.

"Well?" Jake coaxed.

"I want assurances."

"You're in no position to ask for anything."

"I *want* assurances."

"Of?"

"You're not the law here. I want you to promise you'll hear me out."

"That's why I'm here."

"And . . ." She hesitated, her uncertainty seeming to make it nearly impossible to think clearly. "And," she began again, "I want you to make sure my family gets out of this. All of us."

"Can't do that. Your brother may have shot a cop."

"*All* of us," Elizabeth insisted. "My brother is the least of my concerns. You have to promise."

There was an urgency in her voice that Jake had not heard before. For the first time, he thought he might get the truth from her. Intrigued, he said, "You have my word. I'll do whatever I can."

His sincerity eliminated enough doubt for her to begin. "Were you ever in love?"

"I was."

"Without a happy ending?"

"Without a happy ending."

"I thought so. There was a coldness in your voice when you were telling that story about your wife. I'm sorry for you. Really."

Jake believed her. "It doesn't matter now," he said.

"Love always matters. In a place like Winslow, that can be the only thing that keeps you going." She glanced down at her intertwining fingers. "For others," she said, looking back at Jake, "hate keeps them going. You've heard about my father?"

"Yes."

"What did you hear?"

"That he committed suicide."

She paused cautiously. In a low voice, she said, "My father raped me, Mr. Eaton. He first took me when I was twelve and did with me what he wanted until I was eighteen." The indignity spread across her face and collided in her eyes with shameful anger. "Can you imagine how I felt? Do you have any idea the humiliation I suffered?"

Jake didn't. Like most men, he never could. "Did Lottie know what was happening to you?" he asked.

Elizabeth nodded sadly. "She knew. My mother is a very private woman."

"She couldn't ignore the situation forever," Jake said.

Elizabeth banged her hand down, shaking the table. "My mother did *not* ignore me!"

"I didn't mean—"

"What was she to do in a hellhole like Winslow? Who *could* she turn to?" Elizabeth's expression was as mean and hard as her voice. "I told you before, you know nothing about what's been going on in this village. Only those of us stuck here do."

Jake ducked her anger. Emotional jousting got nowhere, and he knew it. "Why didn't you leave?" he asked.

"And go where?"

"You tell me."

"I *am* telling you. We were stuck here with a sheriff who did nothing to help any of us."

"Then Lottie did speak to Sellers about your father raping you?" Jake asked calmly.

"Of course."

"What happened?"

"Nothing. That's what he always did, unless there was something in it for him."

"And Lottie hated him for it," Jake said, remembering Lottie's rancor toward Sellers at his funeral. It seemed years ago.

"Yes, she hated him. I hated him. And Russell hated him more than anyone."

"Enough to kill him?"

"Ten times over, but he didn't do it. You have to understand the sort of man Russell is to believe that."

"I'm listening."

She seemed momentarily shy. "That's why I asked you before if you'd ever been in love. Russell and I always were. When we were in high school, we ran off together. It seemed like the only way I was ever going to be with Russ and be rid of my father." She picked at her nails as she continued. "My father came after us. It was a terrible sight. He hit Russell and kept hitting him and hitting him until I thought he'd die right at my feet." She picked at her upper lip, her eyes heavy and vacant. "That night, my father said that even if Russell did want to marry me, he'd never give me away to anyone. I was his. The way Sellers looked the other way, I believed him. I thought I'd be trapped here in this rotten little village, never able to get away from my father."

"Unless he was dead?" Jake wondered aloud.

There was no hesitation. "Yes. That's right."

"Did you kill him?" Jake asked.

"No. I wanted to each time he touched me, but I couldn't. And mother was too afraid of him to do it."

"Which leaves Russell."

Elizabeth swallowed, her eyes riveted on Jake. "Can I really trust you? Except for Russell, I don't believe much of what any man says to me. If you turn on us—"

"I gave my word. You don't know me well enough to believe this, but it has value."

She sighed and said solemnly, "Russell saved my life. When the prom was nearly over, he went back to my house to tell my father that I wasn't coming home that night, that I was never coming home again. Russell and I were going to be married and that was that. As usual, Old John had been drinking. He didn't listen well when he was sober. He flew into a rage, yelling at Russell, throwing wild punches at him. When the shouting was over, my father lay at the table bleeding from a bullet wound."

"Supposedly self-inflicted."

"Yes. Russell didn't know what to do. He was just a boy, really. Coming forward seemed like such a big, dangerous step, especially since Sheriff Sellers hadn't been any help to us before. So, Russell made it look like a suicide . . . forging a note and everything." She looked at Jake with hopeful eyes. "At that moment, I thought I was free."

"But Myron Sellers wasn't going to let you off so easily," Jake said knowingly.

"How did you know?"

"I've got a pretty clear picture of Sellers. Plus, Lieutenant Moreau briefed me on the case. He said Sellers was the first officer on the scene. Even Sellers could see through a phony suicide set up by a nineteen-year-old kid," Jake said. "He keeps his mouth shut, screws up enough evidence so nobody really knows what happened, then he has your husband in the palm of his hand."

"Crushing him."

"That explains why, when Sellers needed another driver, Russell was the man."

"That's right. Russell had no choice unless he wanted to stand trial for murder. Myron kept the evidence that proved it wasn't a suicide, and he used it every time he needed something. Russell was like a slave to him. Russell didn't want anything to do with that dumping, but he had to go along or Myron would have turned him in."

"You've just given your husband an excellent motive for killing the sheriff."

"But he didn't!"

"Then who did? Those two clowns in the bedroom?" Jake said, knowing instinctively that they weren't capable. He pulled in a deep breath and looked carefully into Elizabeth's pinpoint eyes. Her defenses were up, her physical strength worn down from one battle too many. "It's futile to try and protect him," Jake warned her. "If he—"

"He didn't!"

"Then who did?" he questioned. Then realization came to him with the clarity of a detailed photograph. Elizabeth recognized the look at once.

"You know, don't you?" she asked softly.

"Maybe," Jake answered, the speculation chilling him. Could he have been so blind about all of this? Was the murderer so close he couldn't see? He fell silent as Lottie's image assembled itself in his memory. There she was, rigid as a rake, glaring down at Myron's coffin with shameless, icy eyes.

The quiet turned uneasily on Elizabeth. She took a deep breath. "Every day she left the inn and walked through the village past the sheriff's office. Every day she wanted to go in and confront him."

"Instead, she went in and killed him." It wasn't a question. "What happened?"

Tears welled in Elizabeth's eyes. Her voice was lost.

"Take your time," Jake said as she collected herself.

She spoke, but her voice was hollow. "The disappearance of Colin Owens triggered it. Then you came around asking all those questions. Lottie was afraid that Myron would run off, little man that he was. She didn't want him to get away from anything. She wanted him to pay." Elizabeth looked at Jake. "He ruined her life. She tried to protect me, to help me, and couldn't, because Myron Sellers was a coward."

A coward and a disgrace, Jake thought but let it pass. "Why did Lottie think Myron was about to run away?" he asked.

"She overheard Myron and Colin talking one morning at the inn. Colin was antsy. He told Myron he was getting out before Mrs. Preston compared some pictures. Mother figured that Myron would be right behind, taking the cowardly way out. She wasn't going to let him walk away. She had to stop him."

Stop him she did, Jake thought as the question that dogged him from the beginning answered itself. The reason Sellers died with more than two thousand dollars in his wallet was because Lottie didn't kill for money. She killed to stop the brooding, to end the anguish deep in the center of her soul.

"Sellers's office was torn apart," Jake told her. "Was Lottie looking for something? Or was that you and Russell?"

Elizabeth eyes showed her surprise. "Why do you ask that?"

"You said Sellers kept evidence about your father's killing. You've also got something that Frazer Woodbine's willing to pay for. It doesn't take a genius to figure that you found one or both in Sellers's papers."

She lowered her eyes. "We searched the place. Russ and I." Her earnest gaze was back on Jake. "We wanted what Myron held over Russell was all. We didn't want anything else. If we had that, Russ would be free."

"Did you find it?"

"Yes. A copy of it."

"And what else?" Jake pressed.

"I told you. Some numbers. Lists of numbers. I don't know what they are."

"What made you think Woodbine would be interested in a list of numbers?" Jake asked.

"They had his name on them. And, Russ and I left Myron's office minutes before two men searched it themselves."

"Woodbine's men?"

She nodded. "Yes."

"How do you know who they worked for?"

"They were there when we delivered the note."

Lucky they let you waltz away, Jake thought. "How much are you asking for?"

"One hundred thousand." Elizabeth seemed uneasy mouthing the words, as if the price of blackmail had somehow gotten higher by their very mention.

Jake looked over at Watson, who hadn't moved from his position near the front door. While Watson kept watch, Jake weighed the situation's intangibles. "Woodbine's not going to let you hold him up then walk away," Jake said to Elizabeth with certainty. "If he's willing to pay for what you've got, it's important to him. If it's that important, he'll be afraid you know what it is."

"But we don't!" she exclaimed.

"Doesn't matter. The point is, he can't take the chance that you do and let you two go free. That's probably why he agreed to meet you at the tower. It's isolated, out of the way. The perfect place to set a trap."

The idea rattled her. "A trap?"

"A trap," Jake repeated, working on the best solution to a bad problem. "You've got to get me in touch with Russell. I'll take the documents and—"

Elizabeth shook her head wildly. "I can't."

A car sped by in the early-morning darkness. Jake thought of Ron and Mickey barreling down the road looking for him.

"Of course you can."

"No," she blurted. "No, I cannot! *I* climb the tower as the signal that everything is all right. When Russell sees that it is, he comes out from hiding. There's no other way to contact him, and the next time I'm to be on the tower is at noon."

"Damn," Jake grumbled, seeing the best option of getting them out of this slipping away. "What if I went after Russell on my own?"

"You'd never find him. He knows those mountains better than anyone. He'll stay hidden until he sees me."

"Seems there's no other option," Jake said flatly. "When he does come out, I'll be there waiting for him."

"There's no need—"

"There's every need if I'm going to get to the bottom of this mess," Jake said, his frustration echoing in his voice. "Listen to me," Jake said firmly. "A needle in a haystack is nothing compared to what I'm looking for on twenty thousand acres. Even if I did find it, there's no guarantee I could prove who was responsible unless I get those papers with Woodbine's name on them. I know you don't understand all of what I'm saying, but believe me, Mrs. Oaks, we need each other right now more than you could imagine." Without hesitation, Jake asked where her real children were.

"With mother at the inn. Why?"

"I want you with her in case Woodbine's men get brave and

swing by. Get whatever you need," he told her, picking up the phone. He punched in the numbers and waited. On the seventh ring, a sleepy voice answered.

"Hel . . . hello?"

"Moreau!" Jake snapped.

"Who is this?"

"Jake Eaton."

"What time is it?" The voice wasn't coming around.

"Just after three."

"Where the hell are you?"

"With Elizabeth Oaks."

"Is her brother there?" He was waking slowly.

"Why?"

"Preliminary lab results are in. Lottie's, Elizabeth's, and Russell's prints are all over Sellers's office. I figure it's just a matter of time before Kenney's turn up."

"Forget Kenney."

"Can't. A state diver found what looks to be the murder weapon today in the river about fifty yards from the inn. My guess is Kenney threw it there after he shot Sellers. We should have some prints soon, then it'll be all over but the party."

"I told you to forget Kenney," Jake said again.

"Why?" Suspicion rose in Moreau's voice. "D'you know something I don't? That why you're calling at this hour? What is it, Eaton? Out with it."

"I want you to check on something."

Moreau still sounded skeptical. "Check on what?"

"Find out who did the lab work for Colin Owens."

"The what?"

"Who developed the film? Who processed the negatives? Made the prints."

"Yeah, yeah, yeah." Moreau sounded impatient.

"And Lieutenant," Jake cautioned, "see if whoever did the lab work has any experience in touching up the finished product."

"Every lab enhances pictures, Eaton."

"Not for an aerial surveyor who lies to his clients, who airbrushes things like a drilling rig out of the picture," Jake said.

Moreau's voice climbed a notch. "What? What the hell are you getting at?"

"The bottom of the case, Lieutenant. See what you can do, all right?" He didn't wait for an answer and banged down the phone. He turned to Elizabeth. "He's on to Lottie. The state police have found the murder weapon. If Lottie's prints are on it, the game's over."

"What are we going to do?"

Jake thought for a moment. "I want you to take the two heroes in the bedroom to the inn. Lock 'em in my room if you have to, but I want them out of the way. You stay with your mother until you have to leave for the tower. Moreau's probably going to come around. No matter what he says, tell Lottie not to admit to anything. I'm going to the tower."

Elizabeth opened a drawer. "Wait," she said. She dug around and came out with a topographic map. "Russell uses this when he goes hunting," she said as she unfolded it on the kitchen counter and pointed to a series of small black squares. "The village is right here. We're here. This road dead-ends there." Her finger skated along what looked like an old logging road. "The fire tower is at the far end, here."

Jake looked at the contours and the sweeps and turns of the old road. There was something vaguely familiar about it all.

"It looks like the road I saw in the photographs that Owens took of the Preston property," he commented.

"This is the Preston property," Elizabeth said. "The tower's at the top of Preston Mountain." She pressed back against the rails of the kitchen chair, her shoulders hunched in fear of the unknown. "What's going to happen at noon?" she asked

"We're going to be ready," he said. "That's all I know."

Watson paced near the door, waiting for whatever was before them.

— 23 —

Jake escorted Elizabeth, Kenney, and Joey Barns back to the inn. In the empty downstairs breakfast room, he studied the map of Preston Mountain, planning his approach to the fire tower. When he was finished, he went up to his room and checked on Joey Barns and Kenney Ruggles. Joey lay on the bed, eyes fixed on the ceiling. Kenney sat in the corner chair curled up like a pouting kid.

"You boys behaving yourselves?" Jake mocked.

Joey cut him a hard look. "Where's my shotgun?"

"You don't need it here."

"What if Woodbine's men come back? You ever think of that?"

Jake considered. "The gun is in Lottie's apartment. When I'm gone, go get it." Jake shut the door and went down one flight. He was about to knock when Elizabeth opened the door a sliver. Jake could see Lottie sitting in her chair, smothered by a sense of inevitability and guilt.

"How're you holding up?" Jake asked.

Elizabeth managed a slight smile. "All right, I guess."

Jake bobbed his head. He knew she wasn't. "It'll all be over soon."

"Some endings aren't that good."

He didn't argue. "I figure it'll take me a couple of hours, a little more, to get to the tower. If you don't see me right at noon, don't worry. I'll be there."

"I understand."

There was nothing else to say. Jake walked to the lobby and picked up the phone. He punched in Gloria's number, let it ring once, then hung up. Too damn early, he thought. Let her sleep. He held the phone for a moment, thinking of calling her again. He followed his heart. The phone rang twice before Gloria picked it up.

"It's me," Jake said, about to apologize for calling at seven, but Gloria's voice jumped through the line.

"Then it *was* important," she said. "I thought it might be."

"What are you talking about?" Jake said, puzzled.

"My message."

"What message?"

"The one I left with a Mr. Dodge."

"Didn't get it," Jake said, regretting Dodge's deficiencies as an innkeeper.

Gloria didn't wait for an explanation. "I remembered it just after you left," she said. "Woodbine often bought his properties through a trust."

"Go on."

"Last year, before Milly decided to establish a memorial for Oliver, she came very close to selling. All the negotiations were done through the trust's attorneys, so she never actually knew the buyer's name."

"Interesting."

"I thought so. It gets better. The name of the trust is Pine Willow Properties."

"Owned by?" Jake asked.

"That's what I left the message about. I'm meeting Lewis Metcalf this morning. He's going to help me. And, by the way, he said to tell you he'd have that information you wanted today."

Jake was struck by Gloria's growing level of interest. "What info?" Jake asked, distracted.

"Who opened the bank account," she said eagerly. "It'll be my first time inside The Gorham Corporation's headquarters since Nantucket." An awkward silence filled both phones. Gloria broke it. "You don't sound happy for me, Jake. Little steps? Remember?"

"No, no, it's not that," he said, feeling like an umpire under duress. His lip curled at the horrible thought that she might be going too fast, that she might fail and end up worse off. He broke the quiet with a caution. "I can take care of this, Gloria. You don't have to prove anything to me."

As if the nail had been hit squarely, she said, "And to myself?" There was no changing her mind, and Jake knew it. "Be careful." "I will be," she said.

Jake drove with both hands on the wheel, his eyes straight ahead and wide open as he plunged into the mix of known and unknown with calm objectivity. In times of crisis, Jake was at his best.

The Saab skittered along a soft shoulder, spraying gravel and dust into the air. Soon, the blacktop gave way to a narrow rutted lane. He drove on for half a mile and parked in the weeds. He got out, held the door for Watson to jump down, then went to the trunk. He opened it and took out a compass and the map Elizabeth had given him. He double-checked the load of his .44 Magnum and put a dozen extra shells in his pants pocket. He shut the trunk and locked the car. After checking his watch to mark the time, he and Watson were off.

The trail—rocky and rutted with occasional flat spots—was wide enough to walk on and easy to follow. Jake started slowly, then stretched the pace to a fast walk, propelling himself into a jog on the downward slopes. Watson could keep up with an easy trot, but he ran half the time to make up for sniffing at trees and dashing madly into the thick brush after anything wild.

In half an hour, they were well into the climb. Although the trail switched back on itself to lessen the pitch, the going was still intense, steep, and rocky. Jake leaned into the mountain to keep his pace, steamy breath clouding evenly from his mouth in the cool mountain air. He was sweating lightly, enjoying the stretch of his hamstrings, the crisp coolness of the morning air. For a moment, his mind wandered, and he saw himself in another time, on another mountain.

He was hunting deer with his brother. It was early winter. Ice beaded the tips of weeds and snow clung to branches as they waited in silence for a buck to graze into the clearing. Jake was eighteen and eager to please, but waiting on a cold morning wasn't his idea of hunting. He wanted to stir things up, to go after the deer, to track them, to follow their trails. He wanted to raise his rifle and fire it into the face of life.

But he sat, and soon a small buck wandered aimlessly into the clearing. Max hand-signaled Jake that the prize was his for the taking. Jake raised his rifle, drew the animal into his sights, and fired. The deer wheeled and jumped before staggering backward. Jake saw the flared nostrils, the animal's terrified eyes as it caught itself and for an instant stood frozen. Then, just as quickly, it was off, speeding for the deepest, thickest woods.

It was a clear miss, a clean shot that split bark a foot above the target. Max knew that Jake was a better shot than that and asked why he aimed high.

"Killing him didn't seem necessary," Jake answered. "When I saw him there, when I really looked at him in my sights, I saw how proud and handsome he was. I thought how nice it would be someday if we met again. We could sort of size each other up then, see how we turned out."

Max put his arm around his brother's shoulder in one of those awkward pulling motions, as if he were trying to draw him from boyhood to manhood. "You'll turn out just fine, Jake. You're hard to beat right now."

Jake was brought back to the present by a section of trail surrounded by thick, tall trees with limbs high overhead, cutting out the sun's light. It was like running in a tunnel. The trail snaked around granite outcroppings, then straightened out through a row of pines, birch, and sumac. Finally, he and Watson ran into a clearing. He looked across it and up Preston Mountain until the fire tower appeared.

It was one ridge over and stood on a rounded crest. It looked like something a giant would build with an erector set, complete with switchback stairs, a landing halfway up, and an enclosed hut perched on top.

Jake stopped to look at the map. He'd come nearly halfway in less than an hour. Then he was off again, his mind and body revved up, working as one, as if he were designed specifically to run through the woods on cool spring mornings.

Maybe all those miles of college track were now paying off. Pace . . . rhythm . . . pace . . . rhythm. Swing the arms. Drive with the legs. Breathe. Pace . . . rhythm . . . pace . . . rhythm. On the backswing, his right arm chafed against the handle of the Magnum riding in a holster strapped to his lower back. Pace . . . rhythm. Pace . . . rhythm. He felt as though he could run forever. But then he stopped dead when he saw Watson pull up, both ears cocked like small radar screens.

Watson scanned left, then right. Seconds later, Jake heard it, too—the groan of an overworked engine that sounded as though it was coming from all directions. Quickly, they scurried off the trail to higher ground and listened again. The engine noise faded in and out muffled by trees and valleys.

Jake climbed higher still, looking for a vantage point that would let him see the vehicle, but the forest was too thick. He pulled himself up and perched on a tree limb. He felt vulnerable, exposed. He was playing his game but on Russell Oaks's court, and Russell didn't know they were on the same side.

Jake looked around but saw nothing. He climbed higher, then he saw it. Dust plumes squirreled behind a pickup as it slammed up and down as if bouncing through a minefield. The truck was headed away from him, up the side of the next slope, in the direction of the tower.

Jake eased himself down the tree trunk, then jumped to the ground. He was suddenly tired, arms and legs weary, but he pushed on harder than ever.

Officer Slocum drove toward the inn. Lieutenant Moreau sat in the passenger's seat basking in the glow of near certain victory. Not that he'd actually done anything. The state police had sent the diver who fought the current and found the .22-caliber rifle. Still, Moreau would take what he could, if only to prove to Milly Preston that he was as good as any private detective she hired. But he couldn't let his emotions get the better of him. Hard as they were to shut down, he tried to sound calm, professional.

"Be a hell of a thing, wouldn't it?" Moreau said to John Slocum, who was equally pumped. "I mean, us going in there and making an arrest that will hold up in court. I mean, it'd be one hell of a thing to just catch us a real killer."

"A cop killer, Lieutenant. And, yes, sir, it would be fantastic."

"And who would've thought it was just some punk kid. How do you figure?"

Slocum cut Moreau a quick look. "We've got to get verification on the rifle prints, Lieutenant."

"I know what we have to get!" Moreau's voice jumped out of him. "Sorry. It's just that I feel this in my very bones." He thumped his chest. "Clear down in here, I can feel it. Those prints'll be a match. Kenney Ruggles is guilty as hell, and you know it."

"I hope so. Still, jumping to conclusions . . ."

Moreau gave Slocum a nasty look. "Myron Sellers was one of our own. Don't forget. One of our own. We're under an obligation to find his killer and bring him in. That's exactly what we're going to do." He looked at his driver. "We're just doing our job. Remember that."

"I will, sir," Slocum said proudly.

Moreau felt bigger than life. So this is what it feels like to zoom down the road toward danger. Damn. Nothing to it. Nothing, he thought. "Turn on the flashers, but no siren."

Slocum did as he was told, and the cruiser—flashers blinking in the early morning light—whisked down the highway. In minutes it screeched to a halt in front of the Inn at River Bend.

"This is still an investigation, remember," Moreau cautioned. "We'll show Mrs. Ruggles every due respect, but we want her to tell us where her son is. All she's got to do is point us in the right direction. You and I will take it from there. Understood?"

"Understood."

"Still . . . be careful," Moreau said as he led the way up the porch steps.

Danny Dodge, with a look of total disbelief, was standing at the door. "There must be some mistake," he protested.

"I'll tell you what the mistake is, Mr. Dodge. The mistake is underestimating the capability of the Keene police. Milly Preston didn't need to hire any private investigator, and we're here to prove it!" Moreau and Slocum brushed past the innkeeper toward Lottie's apartment.

"Stay here out of the way, Mr. Dodge. You won't get hurt that way," Moreau said as he stepped forward and knocked. "Police officers," he said too loudly, his voice echoing through the empty halls. He knocked again and said more softly, "No need to be alarmed. We just want to ask . . ." Moreau stopped when the door opened.

Elizabeth Oaks stared back at him with a cool, unpleasant expression. Behind her—as stiff and brittle as a frozen tree limb—Lottie stood, looking convinced that this was one more example of how she'd been born unlucky.

Neither woman spoke as Moreau—followed closely by Officer Slocum—entered the small but tidy apartment.

The lieutenant looked around and cleared his throat. "Nice place you got here, Lottie."

"Hasn't changed since yesterday," Lottie said.

"No. No, I guess not. Of course your daughter wasn't here. Did she fill you in on the weapon we dredged out of the river?" Moreau asked.

Elizabeth calmly closed the door. "We don't have to say anything, Lieutenant. Letting you in is generous."

"And we appreciate it, don't we, Slocum?"

"Yes, sir."

"Yes, we do. We certainly do." Moreau felt his confidence growing. If he played his cards right, who knows? He maneuvered around the room as if lost in deep thought. "Your husband wouldn't happen to be around, would he, Mrs. Oaks? . . . Didn't think so. Too bad. We've got a few questions for him, too. Mostly for Kenney, however."

Elizabeth straightened to her full height. "What's my brother got to do with this?"

"Quite a bit, I'd say." Moreau turned to Slocum and asked, "How long do you figure for the lab to have the prints back on the rifle the state police found, John?"

"Tomorrow. Day after at most."

"And the ballistics?"

"Same."

Moreau shrugged. His look went from Lottie to Elizabeth, then back to Lottie. "What's a day or two?" he asked. "We want Kenney now for questioning in the murder of Myron Sellers."

Lottie's knees nearly buckled. "Kenney? Not Ken . . ."

Elizabeth steadied her mother. "Eaton told us to say nothing," she said, her arm around Lottie's waist. "And that's exactly what we're going to do."

"Jake's here?"

"That's not what I said."

Moreau, smiling, turned to Slocum. "Jake even practices law without a license." Then Moreau snapped, "Get Eaton out of bed. We'll see how he likes looking at facts first thing in the morning."

"No!" Elizabeth said.

"No? Why no?"

"He's not here."

"Who is?"

"No one," she said.

"We can always look, Mrs. Oaks. Who's in his room?"

Elizabeth hesitated, then said, "My brother and Joey Barns."

"Kenney? Damned if it ain't like Christmas," the lieutenant cracked. He stepped to the door. "Slocum, you stay here with the ladies. I'll go bring Kenney down."

"Don't, Lieutenant," Elizabeth said. "Joey's got a shotgun."

A chill sank through him. "He's what?"

"For protection against Woodbine's men in case they—"

"Woodbine?" Moreau paused, assessing the danger. "Why would he need to protect himself against Frazer Woodbine?"

Elizabeth looked right through him, saying nothing.

"Just what I thought," Moreau said. "It's stuff Eaton's filled your head with. This is Winslow, New Hampshire, not New York City. We'd all do well to remember our place," Moreau said and moved into the hall. He looked at the stairs and cautiously began his climb.

The confidence that Moreau had felt was diminishing with each step. He forced himself to be positive, to rid himself of the jangling nerves and the disconnected feelings. It was, he said to himself, perfectly natural for a man to be scared. Men in wars admit it. Men on the front lines never duck the truth. It's okay to be scared, just don't be shaky.

For the first time he could remember, he reached down to his belt and unsnapped the leather strap of his holster. He felt the handle of his department-issue .32 and rubbed it until it was warm.

We're friends, he thought to himself. We're old buddies who take care of each other.

He pulled out the revolver and let it hang at his side as he climbed the last few steps. He had the element of surprise, he had all the options, he said to himself. He wondered what it would be like not to be afraid. Not to be so stiff and uneasy that he had to think out each step to the door.

The moment he stopped, he knew everything was all wrong. He hadn't acted fast enough, or thought it through well enough. He hadn't even knocked when the shotgun blast exploded ripping away half the door. The shock threw Moreau against the back wall and down on the floor. His heart thumped in his chest. Why was he still alive? he wondered as the second blast tore into the plaster above his head.

"Lieutenant!" Slocum was running toward him, taking the stairs two by two. "Lieutenant!" Slocum ran wildly down the hall, action movies rolling in his head. This is living! he thought. This is life! This is what it means to be the police officer he'd always wanted to be. Yet his hands were sweaty and the gun was unsteady as he pointed it and fired.

Moreau was frozen in fear. He couldn't even move when Joey Barns kicked out the rest of the door and, in a panic, fired wildly in Slocum's direction.

Slocum jerked backward as if pulled down from behind. The shot kicked Moreau from his daze, and he emptied his gun into Barns's head and side.

Kenney Ruggles stepped into the hall with his hands high above his head. Reflexively, Moreau raised his weapon and fired six more times, each shot clicking on a spent casing. He got to his feet as his stomach pitched and churned. He dropped the revolver and stared blankly at Kenney's white and tightened face.

Neither had a word for what he felt. Neither moved, surrounded by the spectacle of death.

—24—

It was nearly noon when Jake crossed over the logging road, a half mile from the top of Preston Mountain and the fire tower. It had been a grueling trek, taking far longer than he had thought. Still, Jake and Watson pressed on. There was no sign of the pickup or Russell Oaks. The rocky ledge up ahead was Jake's last hope of spotting Russell before he walked into Frazer Woodbine's trap.

Jake ducked, zagged, and struggled to keep his balance as he and Watson raced toward the granite ledge. Watson stayed as close to Jake as possible, dodging the dense and rugged brush that ripped at his snout. They ran another fifty yards before stopping in the shadows of a huge stand of pines. On the other side was the ledge. Between it and the pines ran a narrow stream. Behind it all, the tower rose like a giant wedge against the bright blue morning sky.

With his heart pounding, Jake broke for a crevice in the ledge twenty yards ahead. The crevice slanted forward at about forty degrees before pitching sharply upward near the top. Jake signaled for Watson to stay, but Watson was already headed for the stream.

Tired from the run up the mountain, Jake relied on his upper-body strength to climb the ledge. He wormed his way from side to side in a state of near-perfect balance.

Near the top where the pitch increased, the handholds became better but harder to locate because he couldn't see them. He had to reach high above his head and feel the stone like a blind man. The thought of reaching into a pit of snakes warming themselves on the hot rock was never far from his mind.

Wedged solidly against the rock, he reached up and pulled himself to the top. A clump of scrub birch growing into the stone hid him from view but provided a perfect line of sight to the tower and its surroundings.

Something was wrong when Jake looked up at the tower. It was empty. Where was Elizabeth? Jake wondered, scanning the area. Then he saw the dusty blue pickup off to the right pulled back into the overhanging pine boughs. Behind it was a man bent so low that Jake could see only the butt of a rifle and a profile of his face. A merciless look of dreadful anticipation covered it.

Jake scrambled down the ledge. On the ground, Watson stood, ignoring Jake's command to follow. "Come on," Jake said again and watched Watson bolt toward a pool of standing water. Jake's thoughts were on Woodbine when Watson bent to drink; he tasted the water then lifted his head with the same horrible expression he had after lapping up the red wine. He shook his head violently, scraped his tongue against his teeth, and backed away.

Jake went to the dog's side and knelt at the water's edge. He cupped his hand, collected some rooty- and brackish-smelling water, and knew before he ever took a sip that it was foul.

A cat seemed to claw his insides as he stepped gingerly around in what was clearly a bog. He could not place the acrid chemical odor. The tainted air was all about him, held in by mountains and tall pines.

Jake's stomach knotted, his heart beat in his throat. Was this what Professor Morrison warned him of? Was this evidence of the deadliest assault ever undertaken on the earth?

"Let's go," he told Watson, moving with stronger purpose over the stream on a patchwork of granite stones. The stream ran cold and clear, with no tainted smell. They pulled up behind the remains of a rock wall. Jake signaled Watson with a flick of his right hand. The dog dashed ahead, running swiftly toward the truck. When the man spun around, his attention on the dog, Jake stepped out from behind the wall. The .44 was aimed at the man's chest.

"Not another move," Jake warned. "Put the rifle down."

The man hesitated.

"Put it down," Jake ordered, moving toward him as the rifle hit the ground.

"Who the hell are you?" The voice was raspy, seeping out from tight lips. The man was in his thirties and had dark brown hair and somber brown eyes. In his faded jeans and worn flannel shirt, he looked like he had just returned from a three-day hunting trip without once shaving.

"I take it you're Russell," Jake said.

"And who are you? Another one of Woodbine's men?"

"I'm Jake Eaton." Jake looked quickly around. "What about Woodbine's men?"

Russell ducked his head in the direction of the sitting Watson. "Over there," he said. "Past the fire tower is an old logging road. One of Woodbine's men drove up it half an hour ago. He got out, looked around, and drove back down. I figure Elizabeth saw him and is just waiting for the dust to settle." Russell reached for his rifle. Jake didn't stop him. "Elizabeth said you'd come by the house a few days ago."

Jake's attention was on the fire tower. "You're a hard man to find."

"That's the point. I drove up early this morning in case Woodbine tried something."

"I know," Jake said. "I came up the back way and saw the dust you kicked up."

"The *back* way?"

"Yeah," Jake told him. "I wanted to catch you before you got yourself killed."

Russell's eyes narrowed, pulling his forehead down into a worried shelf. "Killed?" he repeated. "What the hell are you talking about?"

"The way life can be when you play with blackmail. That's what I'm talking about," Jake said, watching the tan Ford crest the rise in the logging road. It inched forward twenty more yards and stopped near the base of the tower.

Russell strained his eyes, blinking back a look of dispair.

Jake motioned Watson closer, whispered instructions to him, and sent him circling left around the tower. "Do they know you're here?" Jake asked, watching Watson dart through the brush.

Russell shook his head. "No. Looking straight on, you can't see the pickup. I made sure of that."

"Let's keep it that way," Jake said, pointing to the rifle. "Can you hit anything with that?"

"I'm a dead shot," Russell boasted.

"A man's not a target," Jake cautioned. "Men move. Men with something to lose shoot back."

Before Russell could speak, the front doors of the Ford opened. Mickey got out, roughly pulling Elizabeth behind him. He shoved her against the car and stood beside her at arm's length. At the same time, Frazer Woodbine got out from the driver's side. As if stopping on a Sunday drive, he brushed the wrinkles from his suit coat with the palm of his hand. Then he looked at the woods surrounding him. "I know you're out there, Russell. I know you can hear me. Your wife has a message for you."

Mickey stepped back—Elizabeth's cue. She took one step, her head turning left, then right. "Russell . . . ?"

Russell surged forward. Jake dragged him back with one strong hand. "Stay put."

"But my wife . . ."

Jake's menacing finger was in Russell's face. "Shut up. Do what I say, when I say. Do you hear me?"

Russell, eyes wide with uncertainty, nodded. Elizabeth's frightened voice once again shouted his name.

"Russ? Russell?"

The heart-stopping thunder of flushed game birds taking wing broke to her left. Jake rolled his eyes skyward, his pulse quickening at the thought that Watson had rousted the birds. Frazer, however, thought differently.

"Grouse," he informed her, mimicking a kill with an imaginary shotgun. "Your lovely voice," he mocked, "likely frightened them. Are you frightened, Mrs. Oaks? You should be. Now, back to business, if you please."

Elizabeth pulled in a lung full of air to steady herself. "We . . ." she began haltingly. "We've made a terrible mistake, Russell."

"Several!" Frazer was talking to the treetops.

Frazer spoke again, but Jake was concentrating on his own plan. "Where's what you're selling?" Jake asked Russell.

Oaks tapped his shirt pocket. "Right here."

"Give it to me."

Russell pulled out a few sheets of folded paper and handed them to Jake. A quick glance showed columns of numbers, too many to count. The only thing that made sense was Frazer's name at the top of each page.

Jake refolded the papers and was about to put them in his pocket when a thought jarred him. He opened the papers one more time, remembering where he'd seen sets of numbers like this before—on Gloria's sailing charts when he'd visited her in Maine.

"Damn," he mumbled to himself, realizing for the first time what he held in his hand. "Woodbine can't let anybody know about this," he said to Russell. "It'll be the end of him."

"What . . . what do we do?" Russell's whisper fluttered.

"You stay put," Jake said, patting the rifle. "Don't even think about a shot unless all hell breaks loose. Understand?"

"What if I . . . ?"

"There's only one 'what if,' and that's what if you hit your wife. That's for you to think about. What I think about is you back here maybe shooting me. I've got enough to worry about, Russell. I don't need to worry about that. Clear?"

Russell nodded.

"Good," Jake said and retreated to the rock wall. He put fifty yards between him and Russell, then climbed over the wall, the Magnum in his right hand. "Afternoon, gentlemen," he said, his stride assured as he walked toward the group. "Lovely day up here on Preston Mountain."

Mickey swallowed his surprise and checked the awkward movement Elizabeth made in Jake's direction. Frazer's toughness showed in his silence.

"Not surprised?" Jake wondered aloud.

Frazer looked in Elizabeth's direction, then back at Jake. "Not surprised," he said. "As a matter of fact, I half expected it after you went through my office. Bad judgment, Mr. Eaton. It's not like you."

Jake shrugged. "Seemed to be a good idea at the time."

"Like taking Russell's place?" Woodbine asked. "Where is he?"

"Safe," Jake answered, looking at Elizabeth. His answer seemed to reassure her. "He's not going to bother either of us," he offered to Woodbine.

"No?"

"No."

"So," Woodbine said, "what do you want?"

"You," Jake said with a calm evenness that only a man who frequently faces danger could manage.

Woodbine's expression was a mix of intrigue and disbelief. "Me?" he queried.

"That's right. You."

"You seem to forget who's being blackmailed, Mr. Eaton. I'm here protecting my interests, that's all. An innocent bystander, you might say."

"Nothing innocent about you, Woodbine."

Frazer stiffened at the verbal challenge.

Jake motioned behind him with a bob of his head. "I found something back there that might interest you."

"Oh?"

"Yeah. Something oozing out of the ground. Something that might make a man in your line of work want to buy the whole mountain just to keep your secret a little longer."

"I don't know what you're talking about," Frazer said defensively. "And if I did, there's no way you can connect anything to me."

"Maybe. Of course, if what you want to buy back from Russell is what I think it is, you might have to come up with a different story."

Frazer crossed his arms over his chest. "And, what do I want to buy back?"

"A list of LAT-LONG coordinates."

Frazer smiled without amusement. "Assuming that's true, so what? Nothing against the law in that."

"No," Jake agreed, enjoying the mental chase. "Not unless you add one other fact—the fact that a clever and resourceful man like yourself might want to locate what he's hidden. Injection wells, maybe? Hundreds of them?"

Woodbine's hands knifed in the air, stopping the conversation.

"All right, Mr. Eaton. Your point is well taken, the one about clever and resourceful. I am both," he said with contempt. "I am also single-minded. What I want, *really* want, I get." He paused a moment, then continued. "What I want, *really* want, right now is to be done with your toying with me." He stepped toward Jake, a wicked grin riding his face. "You don't think I'd come up here without a safe way out, do you, Mr. Eaton? It'd be unthinkable." Frazer let the idea grow for a moment, then said, "Over to your left, behind the second boulder. Ron has had a rifle pointed at Mrs. Oaks since we arrived. You remember Ron. You shot him in the shoulder. I'd imagine that his aim is now on you. What do you think? An opportunity to get even?" It was Frazer's turn to enjoy the chase, and he savored each second.

While Frazer strutted, Jake looked left toward Ron's shooting position. Ron was there all right—hunched down behind a boulder, the rifle resting on top of it, aimed right at him. Jake strained his sight past Ron, hunting for the stalking Watson. Jake caught a glimpse of him—his back legs slung low—inching toward Ron like a giant cat. It was a comforting sight.

"Toss down your gun, Mr. Eaton," Frazer ordered. "Do it or somebody gets hurt. The lady, maybe. Who knows?"

Jake held the .44 tighter, looking at Mickey, then Frazer, for some hint that neither had the stomach for what was about to happen. He saw no weakness, no nervous tick, so he tossed the Magnum in front of him.

"The best-laid plans," Frazer commented, kicking the gun farther away. Mickey went to pick it up and stopped when Frazer waved him off. "No need for anyone's fingerprints other than Eaton's. Stay with the girl."

Mickey did as he was told, cutting Jake a hateful look. "Where's your fucking dog?" he asked, remembering how Watson pinned him to the chair in Woodbine's office.

"Yes," Frazer agreed, turning to Jake. "Where *is* your dog?"

"Sick."

"Oh?"

"Back down the trail. Seems he drank some of your poisoned water."

Frazer didn't take the bait. Instead, he shrugged it off with a smile. "Those papers," he said finally. "I want them."

"And if you don't get them?" Jake asked, buying Watson more time.

Frazer rolled his hands over and studied his palms. "Two bodies buried on twenty thousand acres would be impossible to find, especially when no one was looking for bodies at all. I'll simply report the blackmail and the payoff. As far as the police will know, Mr. and Mrs. Oaks are fugitives living on my money."

"And me?"

"A tragic victim. I'll say I hired you to get back what was mine. You were shot in the course of doing your job. I'll make sure your eulogy is fitting. Nothing but the best for you, Jake. Now," Frazer said, his tone more serious, "I want those papers."

Jake did nothing. If he gave them up, his life would be over.

Frazer nodded, understanding. "I know the feeling. But I only have to give Ron the word and he'll do what he's paid to do. Nothing personal. It's just business."

"Like your arrangement with Sellers and Owens," Jake said, giving Watson a few more precious seconds.

Frazer looked momentarily annoyed. "Is that what it takes to get you to go along? All right," he admitted. "Colin did occasional jobs for me."

"And Sellers?" Jake asked.

"Both of them. Yes. Nothing illegal about that."

"Depends on what they were doing."

"They kept their eyes open, Jake. Their eyes open and their mouths shut. Perfect employees, you might say."

"Until Mildreth Preston hired Colin to fly a simple survey. What went wrong?"

"All these questions," Frazer said, looking faintly mischievous and shaking his head. "They'll do you no good because I can't afford to answer them. Now, those papers. Please."

Jake made eye contact with Elizabeth, who breathed in, filling her lungs. She exhaled and pulled slightly away from Mickey. "You okay?" Jake asked.

She nodded faintly. Jake's insides knotted, knowing she was on the emotional edge and could take very little more. He had to do something. His gun was twenty feet away. A move toward it and Ron would start firing. Jake was about to hand over the papers and play it from there when Elizabeth asked in a pitiful wail, "Where is Russell? Where is he?"

"Just hang on," Jake cautioned.

But she couldn't. "I want to see him." She was looking past Jake into the thick woods. "I want—"

Frazer lunged toward her. "I don't give a damn what you want, now stop that whining!" he shouted.

Mickey's fuse was just as short. He slapped Elizabeth across the mouth with the flat of his hand. When her shrill cry reached Russell's ears, all hell broke loose.

"Stop it!" Russell shouted, his eyes filled with fear and hatred. "You can't play games with my wife's life! I won't let you!"

Russell was on a dead run, the rifle jerking wildly with each crazy step. He made it ten yards past his pickup when Ron's first rifle shot rang out and dropped him like a stunned bull. Russell went down clutching his leg, writhing in pain.

Jake scrambled toward Elizabeth, shoving Mickey back out of the way with a rolling block. Mickey went down, struggling for air that had been knocked out of him. Jake sprang to his feet as a second rifle shot slammed into the Ford, missing him by inches. From the corner of his eye, he saw Woodbine dash for the Magnum. Jake ducked down and tore after him, expecting more rifle fire any second. Instead, he heard Watson's savage attack and Ron's frightened voice pleading for mercy.

"Call off the dog! Call off the dog! Somebody, help me!" Ron yelled, backing into the clearing, shielding himself from Watson's lunges with his good arm.

Jake reached his revolver first, but Woodbine, seeing that Ron no longer had the rifle, had already given up. He backed away, letting Elizabeth dash to her husband. Woodbine gestured calmly toward Ron and the dog. "I think Ron's had enough," he said. "Call off the mutt."

Jake reproached Woodbine with a nasty look. "He's my partner," he corrected.

Frazer nodded submissively. "The dog," he said. "Call off your dog. Please."

Jake did.

Frazer locked eyes with the detective. "You don't need that gun," he said.

"Strange," Jake replied. "Thought I did."

When Mickey could stand, Frazer motioned him toward Ron. "Take care of him," he said. "And Mickey? Don't try anything."

Jake felt the victory. "Giving up?" he mocked.

Frazer stiffened. "Not my style, Mr. Eaton. I only play to win."

"Maybe you should take another look," Jake told him. "You lost, Frazer. It's all over."

"Hardly," Woodbine said, walking away.

—25—

Jake heard the siren long before he saw the cruiser's flashing lights roar up the logging road. Moreau was driving and Kenney—hands cuffed behind him—sat pouting in back. Moreau stopped near the base of the fire tower, shifted into park, and sat. The steam was out of him. He gazed distractedly at Woodbine's two guards tied together back to back like an uneven stack of New Hampshire cordwood.

"Ain'tcha gonna question 'em?" Kenney teased. "You're the cop."

"Shut up," barked Moreau.

"Well, you are. Go ask 'em some stupid questions like ya did me."

Moreau turned on him. "Shut your dirty mouth! You hear me? Shut it!"

Kenney didn't say another word.

Moreau wanted air. He threw open the door and got out.

"Over here," Jake called.

Moreau walked toward him, his eyes avoiding the two guards. He clapped his hands and bent down as Watson ran up. A dog is sometimes the perfect solution when you need kindness. Moreau turned to Jake. "Slocum took a shotgun in the stomach. He's alive, but . . ." He paused, looking around. "Seems like you've got your own troubles. What the hell happened?"

"Do you really want to know?"

"Truth is, I don't. All I know is one minute the Oaks woman is

184

at the inn, next minute she's gone. Kenney bastard that he is, said she came up here." Moreau gently pushed Watson away. "Where is she?" he asked.

"At the hospital. Russell took a shot in the leg, but he'll be okay."

"And Elizabeth?"

"She's fine, Lieutenant."

"Yeah, well . . ." Moreau seemed lost. Finally, he said, "I see Frazer's men. Where's the man himself?"

Jake pointed toward a crumbling rock wall where Frazer sat. "He's over there. Want to talk to him?"

"About what?"

"Attempted murder, for starters. Maybe something much worse."

"What could be worse?"

"What's happened up here on this mountain." Jake started to leave when the lieutenant held him back.

"It should've been me, you know?" He was looking at the ground, kicking dirt. "I was standing right outside Joey Barns's door. It was one of those moments we small-town cops dream about. All the good the law stands for right there in that moment. I should've known it was all wrong. I *did* know. But I didn't react. I just went down against the wall. I just went down and stayed there," he said, looking disgusted with himself. "If Slocum dies because I didn't do my job . . ."

"There are risks, Lieutenant. You took one. Both of you." They started walking slowly toward Woodbine.

"Sure we did, like two kids. Roaring down the highway, lights flashing on the way to stare down some punk kid. Big men we were." Moreau looked up at Jake, a deep hurt in his eyes. "You warned us to be careful. You called it and I turned the other way to lead the charge. It was so easy to fool ourselves. The blood starts pumping, your hand's on the gun, you're about to save the day. Somebody should have told Joey Barns what the script was. I killed him, Jake." Moreau's entire body sagged. "I'm turning in my badge. I don't ever want to experience again what I went through this morning. Never."

They were in front of Woodbine now. He sat looking at them, his hands on his knees. "I don't believe I've had the honor," Woodbine mocked the lieutenant.

Jake waited for Moreau to put Woodbine in his place, but Moreau was a whipped dog, waiting and watching to be struck again. Without speaking, Moreau turned back toward the squad car.

"Lieutenant?" Jake said after him.

Moreau said nothing, walking with his burdens, ignoring the black dog at his side.

Jake faced Woodbine, oddly curious at the man's calm demeanor.

Frazer read the look in Jake's eyes. "You've got nothing on me, Eaton. I could sit here all day watching you drum up charges, but nothing—*nothing*—is going to stick."

"You seem damn sure of yourself."

"Just like you. And how did we get this way? We play the game holding the aces. We play to win. There is no other way."

"Even if it means killing Oaks and his wife?"

Frazer waved off the question with a flip of the hand. "Means nothing. I'm telling you, Jake, forget it."

"Why should I?"

"Because," Frazer said with a smile, "I'm holding five aces." He spread his fingers. "Count 'em."

Jake reached out and grabbed Frazer's open hand. He closed it, held it tight, and slowly, carefully applied more pressure.

"I could break every finger," Jake warned, torquing his grip. "Every finger in your greedy little hand."

For the first time, Frazer lost his flair. "I know you could." He gritted his teeth. "I know you could, but that would be a mistake."

Jake squeezed to the breaking point. Frazer cried out and Jake let go. "What's the fifth ace?" Jake demanded. "What are you holding?"

"Not a what, a who." Frazer opened and closed his aching fingers. "The boy's going to get crushed, Jake. It's up to you."

"I'm listening."

"You want a story, do you? All right. Once upon a time in a tiny New Hampshire village," he began, "there lived a very mean and nasty man. One night when his daughter and beau came in from a village dance, the very mean and nasty man was killed. The story of a suicide spread throughout the village, and, as is the case with fables, everyone lived happily ever after." Frazer stopped and looked evenly at Jake. "Nice story, don't you think?"

Jake returned the stare. "As far as it goes," he said.

Frazer nodded. "It doesn't quite go far enough, does it, Jake? Say that the long version of the fable takes a turn as mean and nasty as the old man himself. Say the long version proves that the old man didn't kill himself after all. Say the long version names the killer."

"There were extenuating circumstances," Jake said firmly.

Frazer beamed a smile. "Aren't there always? And there were in this case. Two sets of extenuating circumstances; yes, sir, there were. Say the boy had good reason to kill the old man. All right, knock it down to second degree and he gets ten years. But add to that the *second set of circumstances*—extortion—and you kick it back up to—what?—fifty years, maybe?"

Jake felt the noose tighten. "What are you angling for, Frazer?"

"What I wanted to begin with: Mildreth Preston's property and the packet that Russell turned over to you."

"And if Milly won't go along?"

"Then I'll turn Russell in," Woodbine said, the bargaining over. "Russell killed that old man. I've got the evidence to prove it. The *original* documents that Sellers put together telling the truth about what happened that night are in my safe."

"A Christmas present from the sheriff?" Jake spit out, disgusted with the man before him.

"Sellers had his price. I was happy to make him a rich man."

"At what cost to you?" Jake asked. "Someday, you'll have to answer that."

"Perhaps." Woodbine was unflinching. "Until then, consider this. If Mrs. Preston wants to send Russell to prison, she can ignore me. However, I doubt if she wants to spend the rest of her life with Russell Oaks on her conscience. Think about it. Or would you prefer me to have a chat with Lieutenant Moreau right now about a bungled blackmail attempt? Might cheer him up."

Jake swallowed the stinging disgust that was inching up from his insides. Then, suddenly he remembered something and pointed a finger sternly at Woodbine. "Stay right here," he told him and walked the twenty yards back to the lieutenant.

When Jake spoke his name, Moreau acted as if awakened from an unpleasant dream. "Yeah?" he asked, leaning against one fender of his car. "What do you want?"

"Some good news."

"Don't we all," Moreau mused. "Don't think I have any."

"You might if you checked out what I asked you to." Moreau looked puzzled. "The lab," Jake prompted. "The lab where Colin Owens had his film developed. What'd you find out?"

"Not much. It's one of those 'open bay' outfits down in Boston. They'll do all the processing and printing for you, or you can work on your own."

"Did Colin know his way around a darkroom?" Jake asked.

"He did. The man I talked to said Colin was as good as they come at doctoring prints."

Moreau's words were a spark of hope. "Thanks, Lieutenant," Jake said and strode confidently back to Frazer, who watched him all the way.

"What was that about?" Frazer asked nervously.

"A little matter regarding Colin Owens," Jake told him. "Seems he was a very talented man. I can see why you'd pay him so handsomely."

Frazer looked genuinely curious. "Can you, now."

"I can, Frazer," Jake said as a scornful superiority crept into his smile. "I can, and it's going to put you right out of business."

"You don't know what you're talking about," Woodbine countered. "There's no way."

"Ah, but there is. I haven't figured out all of it, but I can make a damn good guess as to what took place on this mountain."

Frazer said nothing, his expression carrying only mild concern.

"There's an injection well here somewhere. Whatever fissure it was bored into has filled up, and now the waste is leaking out onto the surface. Watson and I found a poisoned bog not a hundred yards from here," Jake said. "What happened? Did Colin spot the leaks when he did the flyover?"

"You're out of your mind," Frazer said through a forced smile. "Completely out of your mind."

"I don't think so," Jake responded. "But Colin might have been. He was about to turn over a set of photographs to the wife of the world's best-known environmentalist. Only these weren't just any photos. No, sir. These pictures clearly showed a new, hideous toxic waste site snaking through her land. But, no problem," Jake said facetiously. "All Colin had to do was go to his lab and brush out all evidence of the damage. The problems began when Mildreth noticed that something was wrong. Colin brushed out a contaminated area near a road and put the road back incorrectly. Milly caught that right off. It was the road along one of their favorite walks. She got suspicious and called Colin. Instead of visiting Mrs. Preston with an explanation, Colin disappeared."

"Which, unfortunately, is when you came in," Frazer said, looking at Jake, sharp eyed as a bird. "I had Mickey and Ron follow you around for a few days to see what you were up to."

"And follow Mrs. Owens," Jake said, the memory of her opening a door in his head. He saw the bottle of scotch and two glasses on her kitchen table. "Mickey and Ron paid her a visit before I did," he ventured.

"That's correct. They went to tell her where Colin was staying for a few days."

"And where was that?"

"I have a cabin. He was there, perfectly safe. All he had to do was wait. That's all everyone had to do. Sit tight and wait."

"Until when? Until you had your little meeting with me, and I could go back to Mrs. Preston with another offer for her land?"

"Something like that," Woodbine said.

"But you must've considered the possibility that I'd refuse."

"Oh, I did. I've considered *every* possibility, Jake. Like I said, I'm holding the winning hand. You're the one bluffing."

Slowly, deliberately, Jake removed the papers from his pocket. "Does this look like a bluff to you? Once the coordinates on these pages are checked out, you're done."

"And what do you think they'll prove?" Frazer asked through clenched teeth.

"The location of what you can't see with the naked eye: perfectly covered up injection wells. Hundreds of them. Thousands, maybe. Doesn't matter. The point is, you're finished. Out of business, just like your old man."

"No," Frazer said. "That's where you're wrong. The rules in this business have changed over the years, Eaton. True, my life would be easier if those pages were in my possession. But if you keep them, you've got a handful of nothing.

"Now, I've had enough," he said, brushing past Jake. "Give Milly Preston this message," he demanded. "She sells to me, or I'm throwing Russell Oaks at the feet of the police. It's time to decide."

Frazer wasn't bluffing. Jake looked into the man's narrowing eyes.

"What's it going to be?" Frazer wanted to know.

It was one of the few times Jake hated his work. His job was to gather information and present it. It wasn't to make decisions for his client.

"I'll tell her," he said finally. "I'll tell Mildreth your terms."

"Good." Woodbine's victorious grin made Jake's skin crawl. "Don't look so gloomy, Jake. You said it yourself. I'm clever and resourceful. It's the only way to stay in business."

"You won't be in business long, Woodbine," Jake said, the hollowness of the threat ringing loudly in his ears.

—26—

It was late June when the state of New Hampshire notified Mildreth Gibbon Preston that they wouldn't take the responsibility for her contaminated property. They acknowledged the generous offer, thanked her for her patience, praised her for her vision, then told her she had ninety days to report—in writing—how she was going to clean up the cornucopia of hazardous, toxic, and carcinogenic substances that had been injected into a mile-long fissure in the granite on her property. State geologists estimated that several million gallons of waste remained in the fissure.

The letter from the state seemed to Mildreth like some cruel hoax. The property Oliver loved soaked with poison? When the anger and utter dismay left her, Mildreth had the letter framed as a monument to the vicissitudes of life. She held a small ceremony to hang it. Watson had something special in the kitchen; she, Jake, and Gloria sipped vintage port, a 1968 Vargellas. She held out her glass for a refill and Jake obliged—first Mildreth, then Gloria.

"I hate to admit the possibility," Mildreth said, "but maybe I'm an old fool after all."

"Nonsense," Gloria replied. "The memorial was a wonderful thought."

"Perhaps." Mildreth seemed reluctant to let go of the concept. "I only wish it had turned out better."

"There wasn't much more we could do," Jake admitted, feeling deep inside that he hadn't done all he could.

Mildreth saw his pained look and tried to comfort him. "You did your best," she said. "No one could have done more." Mildreth sipped her port, savoring the warming flavors. "I'm going to suspend Oliver's rule," she said. "I'm going to mention that despicable name: Woodbine."

"Otis Woodbine," Gloria added.

"It was really he who started all this?" Mildreth queried.

"It was," Jake told her. "Along with Colin and Myron. All three were involved in the dumping that Joey Barns started. From the air, Colin would pick out the best land routes for the trucks to follow and remain unnoticed. Myron would identify who'd be away from their property and pick the dump site accordingly. It didn't take long for a man like Otis to see they were on to something. He wanted a piece of the action."

Mildreth said solemnly, "Such a horrible man."

"True, and one willing to take risks." replied Jake. "Who but he would've thought to dig a deep injection well on the property owned by the father of the environmental movement?"

"As I said," Mildreth repeated, "such a horrible man."

Gloria gazed into her glass. "Myron Sellers wasn't much better," she said.

"No," Mildreth agreed, thinking for a moment. "So it really was Lottie who walked into Sellers's office and shot him?"

"Yes," replied Jake.

"That poor family," Mildreth offered. "What Lottie and those children went through. It must've been pure hell."

"Kenney's no prize. He did break into this house with Colin," Jake reminded her. "He did wound a cop."

"And," Gloria added, "he was with Barns when they tried to run Jake down."

"I never did understand that," Mildreth said. "Why would they want to hurt you, Jake?"

"Kenney thought he was helping his sister. The blackmail scheme was in the works as soon as Russell searched the sheriff's office and found those papers. Kenney thought I'd stumble onto it and ruin their chance at the money."

"And Kenney's connection with Owens?" Mildreth wondered aloud.

Jake shrugged. "The kid was like a pinball in an arcade. He bounced from bad idea to bad idea. Colin was just another."

"What will happen to Kenney?" Gloria asked.

"First offense. Hard to say."

Mildreth stiffened. "I will admit," she said, "that I don't much like the boy; still, I think they've suffered enough. That Russell. It's as though he's been tortured all his adult life."

"In a way, he has been," Jake agreed. "Otis Woodbine was shrewd. He wouldn't take the chance of joining up with Colin and Myron until Barns's small-time operation was shut down. Somebody had to take the fall so everyone would be convinced that the Winslow dumping was over. Myron arrested Russell to set up the phony trial so everybody would think that the dumpers had been run out of town. Before you knew it, they were back in business. Only this time, Otis was at the helm—until his luck ran out and *he* was finally put out of business."

"It's disgusting," Mildreth said sadly.

"And ingenious," Jake said. "When Frazer came along, he added technology and brought the business into the twentieth century."

"I still don't understand the significance of the packet that Frazer wanted to buy back," Mildreth said. "I understand flight coordinates, but you haven't told me why they were so important."

Gloria glanced at Jake, a look so telling, that Mildreth picked up on its importance.

"What is it?" she asked, then coaxed, "Gloria? Jake? What aren't you telling me?"

Jake leaned forward in his seat. "They're other sites," he said, his voice grim. "Other deep wells dug all around the country."

Mildreth mouthed the words, her voice a mere whisper. "Other sites?" she said. "How many?"

"Hundreds. Over a thousand, maybe. The exact count can't be made until the wells are actually located. As you know," Jake reminded her, "that's not easy."

"A thousand . . ." Mildreth's voice trailed off. "And as on my land, they fill up, and whatever's been poured down in them eventually runs out, poisoning everything around them?"

Jake regretted the answer before he said it. "Eventually."

Mildreth's free hand slammed the arm of her chair. "Then why isn't Frazer Woodbine in jail? Why?" she demanded.

Jake waited for Mildreth to calm down. "We could always say no to the deal. It's your call. Russell's not a choirboy. He did kill a man."

"I know what he did!" Mildreth fired back. "This . . . this entire situation is appalling. Horrible men, horrible times, horrible. I don't like anything about it. Not one thing!"

"It's not a perfect world, Mrs. Preston."

"No, it's not, Mr. Eaton." Mildreth glared at him. "Frazer Woodbine will walk away without even a slap on the wrist. He's responsible for toxic waste sites all over this country? Thousands, maybe." The number rattled her. "That man," she snapped, "belongs behind bars!"

"So did Al Capone," Jake reminded her. "But Capone never went to jail for his major crimes. He was convicted of tax evasion."

"What is your point?"

"You tell her, Gloria. You did the work on it."

Mildreth sounded irritable. "On what?" she wanted to know.

"On Pine Willow," Gloria said. "Pine Willow Properties owns the land the illegal wells are on. Because Pine Willow is a trust, there's no direct connection between it and Frazer Woodbine."

"None," Jake agreed. "At least none I could find. But Frazer did make one mistake. He opened the account that Myron Sellers and Colin Owens used at Harbor National. It's a money trail that leads directly to Frazer and ChemTrol's deep pockets. Deep pockets that may lead to real estate deals through out the country."

Mildreth sensed a speck of justice. "Then you *can* bring him down?"

"Like I said, taxes tripped up Al Capone. Maybe a bank account will undo Frazer Woodbine. He may not spend the rest of his life in jail, but an investigation into his connections between a crooked sheriff and a bogus surveyor ought to slow him down, give him something to think about. But," Jake warned, "if you give the okay and I go after him, you know what will happen."

Mildreth stood, pulling in lungs full of air, stretching herself to her full height as she did so. "I do." She let out the air, saying,

"I can throw away the life of Russell Oaks and his family." She put down her port glass and walked toward the dollhouse as she spoke. "Do you remember the conversation we had at the inn, Jake? I was telling you that changes had come over Oliver once we'd bought that mountain." Mildreth turned toward Jake. "I told you that Oliver was holding something back from me, and that he'd never done that before." She cut her eyes toward Gloria, looking embarrassed at what she was about to say. "I also told you how much I disliked Russell Oaks. I may have said I hated him for being a hauler on our land. Do you remember what you said to me?"

"I do."

"What was it?"

"Since Oliver loved the world, I asked if he might not be more generous."

"What you meant was, more generous than I in his ability to forgive."

Jake nodded. "That's what I meant," he said.

Mildreth sighed "As I think back on it, I've come to believe that what Oliver kept from me was Russell's terrible secret. I believe that Oliver knew Russell had killed Old John. How he knew, I'm not sure. Perhaps Myron told him or, more likely, threatened him with the knowledge when Oliver was himself threatening to take all the dumpers, every last one, to trial. Does that make sense to either of you?" she asked.

"It could," Jake offered. "Joey Barns told me that Oliver and Sellers argued about something. Next thing Joey knew, Oliver agreed not to take the case to court."

"Oliver protected Russell?" Gloria questioned.

"Yes," Mildreth said. "I think that's exactly what he did."

"Then why not admit it to you?" Gloria asked.

"Because, as Jake so rightfully pointed out, back then I was not so generous, not so willing to forgive. Maybe keeping Russell's secret is the best memorial I could offer my husband."

"And what about Oliver's reputation as an environmentalist? Can you live knowing that Woodbine has gone free?" Jake asked.

"The question is," Mildreth said, "can I live knowing I let Frazer

Woodbine ruin one more living thing? Russell, Elizabeth, and Lottie are faces I see in my dreams. I can't toss their lives away. If Oliver didn't, how can I?"

Jake let what he'd just heard sink in. "No one can tell you what's best, Mrs. Preston. You're damned if you do and damned if you don't."

"What would you do, Jake?" she asked.

"I don't know. Life's full of those situations where you never know until it's your time to act. All I can say is, it's not my time."

Mildreth knew he was right. She turned to Gloria and asked the same question.

Gloria's eyes sparkled. "You do what you can live with," she said. "That's what Lieutenant Moreau did when he resigned from the force."

"Even though Slocum lived," Jake said. "That surprised me. Had he died, I figured Moreau was out of there, but not the other way."

"Did you think the lieutenant would turn Lottie in?" Gloria asked.

"I did. Instead, he turned in his badge and a final report on the case. Not enough evidence to bring charges, he said. Lottie's off scot-free."

"Speaking of free," Gloria said. "How did Sellers explain all that money he and Owens got?"

"He didn't have to explain it," Jake said. "That was the whole point of the card games. Colin arrives with some of the payoff and hands it over to Myron at the card table. No questions asked," Jake said as Watson sauntered in from the kitchen, looking full and licking his chops. He stretched out on the Persian rug, apparently satisfied.

"I think he liked his snack," Gloria said, smiling.

"I'd say so."

"I don't suppose you'd like to let him stay here?"Mildreth asked Jake.

"No."

"I don't blame you," she said, walking back to her glass of port and picking it up. "Well, I believe it's time for the ceremony."

Jake and Gloria stood. Gloria picked up the framed letter and gave it to Mildreth.

Mildreth took it and walked steadily to the wall opposite the dollhouse. She motioned toward the hammer and picture hook.

"Would you care to do the honors, Mr. Eaton?"

"It would be a pleasure, Mrs. Preston."

Jake took the hammer and tapped the small nail into the plaster where Mildreth Gibbon Preston indicated. She handed Jake the framed letter and stepped back while he hung it.

"A bit to the left," she urged. "Perfect." She stood rigidly as if she were about to salute. Her chin wrinkled and she fought back her tears. "I don't mean to seem unkind, but it isn't perfect at all, is it? It's quite the opposite."

Gloria stepped toward her and put her arm around Mildreth's shoulder. "It's all right, Milly."

Tears spilled from Mildreth's eyes. "I don't know," she said, wiping her cheeks. "I don't."

"Neither did I until Jake asked for my help. I said no, then finally I took one little step. You might say that Oliver's memorial saved two lives: Russell's and mine."

Mildreth hugged Gloria, thanked her, and stepped away, inhaling deeply. She turned to Jake. "Well, I suppose we should get on with it. As I said to you before, Mr. Eaton, there comes a time in life when even on our best days we have to admit that things will not improve."

They clicked glasses.

"This is one of those days. A toast," Mildreth said, "to a once perfect place."